"Arellano has created a brilliant novel of political satire ...
His over-the-top debauchery is both comical and charm-
ing ... and never lets the reader down. Recommended."
—*Library Journal*

"Fear and loathing with Don Quixote at your side!
Herein another savage journey to the heart of the Ameri-
can dream—but with *sabor* and *saber latino*."
—Ilan Stavans, author of
Spanglish: The Making of a New American Language

"This book is like a good fistfight: You get punched and
kicked but you still want more."
—Daniel Chavarría, author of *Adios Muchachos*

"A raucously funny satire of machine politics wrapped up
in a parody of *Don Quixote* ..." —*Chicago Reader*

"Robert Arellano's new book is one of the bawdiest, dirti-
est, rowdiest, and raunchiest novels I've come across in a
long time. And it is hilarious. Hurling words like tainted
pitchforks, he pursues his wanton prey as if on speed himself, snort by snort, sexual escapade by sexual escapade, as
Don Dimaio lays waste to the city he's supposed to govern
... This boisterous cartoon of a book captures the obses-
sions and mad fantasies of men running amuck, Dimaio
on power, Arellano on language ... Don Dimaio is an anti-
hero for all ages ..." —*Providence Sunday Journal*

"I hope that the author is not killed for writing this book.
A municipal fornicator (pot) shines a waterfire light deep

into the more-than-half-full actions of a civil servant (kettle). So between the writer and his protagonist, a new meaning of 'black' power arises."

—Will Oldham of the Palace Brothers

for *Fast Eddie, King of the Bees*

"The main story here is the author's style, which takes its cue from William S. Burroughs, Philip K. Dick, Charles Dickens, Jack Kerouac, and Tom Robbins. This may be the first postapocalyptic novel in which the apocalypse was created by a public works project . . . [A] funny and surprising book."

—*Library Journal*

"Robert Arellano is that rare thing: an exceptional creative talent perfectly in tune with his own rapidly changing times."

—Robert Coover, author of *Noir*

"A rollicking, over-the-top, not to mention weird, odyssey . . . *Fast Eddie* is a Dickensian journey on speed, several years into this new century, where society is decayed, deregulated and Darwinianly desperate . . . Deliriously funny . . ."

—*Providence Journal*

"A tight close-up, mile-a-minute monkey-cam filled with more wordplays and puns than an Eminem rap."

—Arthur Nersesian, author of *The Swing Voter of Staten Island*

"*Fast Eddie* is an Oedipal story with a twist . . . This is surrealist fiction, a bit Kafkaesque . . ."

—*Columbia Chronicle* (Chicago)

Jeanine Tasso

ROBERT ARELLANO'S parents fled Havana in 1960. He has been working on *Havana Lunar* since 1992 when, as a student in Brown University's graduate writing program, he visited Cuba on a research fellowship. He has returned ten times, chronicling the Revolution in journalism, essay, and song. He is the author of two other highly acclaimed novels, *Fast Eddie: King of the Bees*, and *Don Dimaio of La Plata*, both published by Akashic Books.

Havana Lunar

Robert Arellano

AKASHIC BOOKS
NEW YORK

The author is grateful for permissions from the *Indiana Review* and the *Believer*, who published early versions of excerpts from this novel.

Published by Akashic Books
©2009 Robert Arellano

ISBN-13: 978-1-933354-68-2
Library of Congress Control Number: 2008925931

First printing

Akashic Books
PO Box 1456
New York, NY 10009
info@akashicbooks.com
www.akashicbooks.com

For Tom & Jane Lee Carr

14 August 1992

It's Friday, and when I get back to the attic I see that Julia hasn't returned. I sit on the sofa, light a cigarette, and turn on the radio, tuning out the noise of the neighbors with the hollow metronome of Radio Reloj. *"Did you know that good nutrition can be obtained from greens you can grow in your own solarium . . . ?"* I don't want to be up in the hot attic with the tedious banter and the beginning of a migraine, so I go downstairs and let myself into the clinic to lie on a cot. When my grandmother Mamamá died, the Reforma Urbana "reallocated" the lower floors of my father's house: the first to a family from the provinces and the second to Beatrice, the block captain for the Comité de Defensa de la Revolución, whose eye, as the CDR symbol suggests, is always open. I had to set up a community polyclinic in the basement just to dig my heels in and hang onto the attic. Three weekends a month, legitimate cases of arthritis and herpes vie for attention with the usual complaints of mysterious pains and aches from patients who believe the only remedy is a shot of painkillers. It makes them feel a little better when they hold a doctor's attention. I listen, letting them speak for the adrenal rush it gives them, and then I explain for the thousandth time that it is the Special Period: There is no more morphine, not even aspirin.

Alone in the empty clinic at dusk, I am resting in one of the curtained compartments when a thunderstorm breaks the heat. The shower passes quickly, briefly taking my migraine away and leaving the street outside quiet, clean, and fragrant of motor oil and rotting leaves.

I am listening to the dripping trees when I hear the crack of glass. A gentle pressure like a cold hand causes the hairs on my neck to stand, and I experience a surge of obscure fright. I part the curtain to peer at the front door of the clinic, where a gloved hand reaches through a broken windowpane and releases the lock. *¿Qué carajo?* It's common knowledge the neighborhood doctors don't have any more drugs, but a heavyset man in a dark overcoat is breaking into my clinic. He makes straight for the metal file cabinet, and I lie still, watching around the edge of the curtain. The man flips through the charts for a few minutes and leaves the clinic without taking anything, closing the door behind him. I go out through the alley and come around the front of the building to see him walking away up Calle 23. I follow him at a distance through the rain-slicked streets.

There is a hush over Havana. The moon, almost full, is rising above the bay. It is high summer, when the palms drop curled fronds that pile up on sidewalks like brittle cigars. Sidestepping them, I keep the overcoat in sight. I follow the man up Infanta all the way to La Habana Vieja and down one of El Barrio Chino's narrow, nameless alleys. He disappears through an unnumbered entrance. No light leaks from the door glass, painted black.

I slip inside the corridor and push apart the dark drapes onto a small drinking establishment. A black bartender pours beer from a tap. Sitting at the bar with his back to me, the man in the overcoat says, "Give Doctor Rodriguez one on me." Surprised, I step out of the shadows. The man who broke into my clinic casts a glance over his shoulder to confirm my identity, looking blandly at the contusion beneath my right eye, a port-wine stain the size of a twenty-peso coin. His deep lines, pale complexion, silver hair, and mustache mark him as an autocrat of the Fidelista generation. The gray eyes and dark brow could almost be called handsome if his expression were not so stern and inscrutable. "Please have a seat, doctor. My name is Perez."

There is nobody else at the bar, but I keep an empty stool between us. "That's very humble of you, colonel. Anyone who reads *Granma* knows who you are."

"What will it be?" the bartender asks.

"Do you have wine?"

"I've just uncorked a very good five-year-old Chilean Cabernet." The bartender shows me the ornate label. "Or if you prefer I'm chilling an excellent Pinot Grigio de Venezia."

"The Cabernet will be fine, thanks."

The bartender places a glass before me and pours a generous serving. I take a taste, but the pounding of my heart and a sour flavor in my mouth keep me from enjoying it. "Tell me, Colonel Perez, what interest could the chief homicide investigator of the PNR possibly have in a pediatrician with the national medical service?"

He sips the fresh-poured beer. "I'm looking for a teenage girl wanted in connection with the murder of a chulo named Alejandro Martínez."

"¿Cómo?"

"The young woman in question spent a week at your apartment, and the victim came over and threatened both of you a few days before his body got tangled up in some fisherman's nets at the mouth of Havana Harbor."

"Could it have been accidental, a drowning?"

"There were signs of struggle: lesions on his

arms and chest. Of course, the exact cause of death has been difficult to determine as we still haven't found his head."

"Carajo . . ."

"He was not especially popular among the girls." Detective Perez takes off his gloves. His fingers are exquisitely manicured. Only once before, when I was starting medical school, have I seen such hands on a man. They belonged to the cadaver inside which I saw my first organs.

"Severing the cervical vertebrae requires both the right instrument and great force," I say, "not to mention a strong stomach and a lot of nerve. A girl couldn't have done that."

"Young ladies come from all over the island to work in Havana, doctor. Some will spend a few months, others a year or two, do a few dirty things, and usually they will go back to their villages and shack up with campesinos, have kids, lead normal lives. But there is another type. Surely you know the constitution: the solipsist. No matter what she gets in this life, she believes she deserves more." Perez swallows the last of his beer and rises to go. "If you see the girl again, I'd like you to contact me. Come back and talk to Samson, the bartender."

"You choose unusual locations to conduct your inquiries, colonel."

"Stay reachable for a few days, doctor. Don't

leave Havana." Perez parts the drapes and is gone. I wait a minute before leaving, neglecting to finish my glass of wine. Samson does not look up.

I return home to Vedado and pull Aurora's old rocking chair close to the French doors, parting the curtains onto the corner of 12 y 23: the bored soldiers, the old Chevys, the people going by and, across the street, a black Toyota with dark windows, a curl of smoke emerging from the passenger side. Taking the service stairs down, I back the Lada out of the garage and leave it parked in the alley. When I check on the basement clinic, the broken window-pane has already been replaced.

31 July 1992

T'wo weeks ago, my Friday shift at the pediatric hospital was almost over when Director González stepped around the curtain and handed me an envelope with my week's pay. "Rodriguez, you have tomorrow off, don't you?" Director González has always cultivated a studied, comfortable air toward my mark.

"Sí, señor."

"Would you stay over? Portuondo's bus was canceled."

"Sí, señor."

The admitting nurse briefed me on the next patient. "Una niña, ten years old, complaining of fever and an earache; high temperature, blurry vision, and slightly slurred speech."

Holding her mother's hand, the girl sat on a bench in the sala de examinación, a four-by-five compartment partitioned by plastic curtains strung up in the hot, drafty lobby. "First the earache," said the girl's mother. "Then the fever started. We waited a few days to come in."

"How many days, exactly, since the onset of the fever?"

"Four."

"Cuál es tu nombre, amiguita?"

"Me llamo Tonia."

I asked Tonia's mother, "Does your daughter have a speech impediment?"

"No."

"Tonia, can you tell me how many animals you count on the curtain there?"

"The light hurts." Her slur was pronounced. She focused on the mark beneath my right eye. "What's that on your face?"

"A bird dropped it on me." I turned and asked the mother, "Is anyone else with you?"

"My husband is in the waiting room."

My first task of the second shift was to convince Tonia's father that the girl's ailment was a lot more serious than a simple ear infection. Both of the girl's parents sat across from me at the desk I shared with four other pediatricians. "Your daughter has to stay here tonight."

The father stared suspiciously at my mark. "Come on, doctor. Just give the girl a shot and we'll be gone."

"She might have a cerebral abscess. She needs to be under close observation. This could require massive antibiotics."

"We live right around the corner in the Máximo Gomez apartments."

"You can spend the night in her room, if you'd like, but Tonia has to stay."

The father stood up and left the office, slamming the door behind him. The mother looked at me. "Do you have any children, doctor?"

"No," I said. I try to take care of every patient as if she were my own child, but to tell a parent this would just irritate the situation.

"If you let my baby die, you will be killing me too."

"I will do everything in my power to help your daughter."

"Imagine if your own mother had lost you, how she might feel."

There is no more powerful antidote than a mother's will for her child's survival. Sometimes this takes the form of a bitter pill, a country woman suspicious of all the gleaming machines and of their handlers, the doctors and nurses. Then there are those who trust modern practices. Either way it is a welcome medicine when a parent's stubbornness overpowers a child's fear.

I gave the nurse instructions to admit Tonia to

intensive care and asked an orderly to set up a cot for the mother beside the girl's bed. Then I walked down the hall to the physician's lounge, a small, windowless closet with a bare bulb on the back wall and a dusty jug of water for refreshment. The coffeemaker had been stolen during the second week of my residency, and nobody had bothered filing a report because it had been a year since they had stocked coffee. Sometimes, in the middle of a double shift, I'll go there to stretch my legs across two plastic chairs and catch a short nap.

Tonia's father pushed the door open without knocking. "What are you doing in here?"

"Taking a siesta."

"Nothing is happening. Why can't I take my daughter home?"

"Please, get some sleep yourself. They made up an extra bed in her room."

"I don't like a bed. I sleep on a bench."

A nurse interrupted. "Doctor Rodriguez, venga pronto."

I pushed past the father and ran down the hall to Tonia's bed. I had been planning to order a CT scan in the morning, hoping there would still be time to go with a sequence of antimicrobials, but now Tonia's condition had become critical. The abscess was hemorrhaging. I told the head nurse to prep the OR for emergency surgery and went in to scrub up.

After the anesthesiologist put the girl under and the intern shaved the area over the abscess, I made an exploratory incision with the scalpel. Fortunately, I found the mass near the surface and completely encapsulated by membrane. Excision was completed quickly and without complications. I took a culture of the residual fluid with an aspirator and asked the intern to sew the patient up and send her on to post-op. Then I requisitioned the biopsy exam and wrote up a preliminary convalescing plan, treatment to be adjusted upon identification of the infecting microorganism.

By the end of the shift, Tonia was stable in the ICU. I informed Tonia's parents that surgery had been successful and that I expected the girl's complete recovery in a matter of days. Candelario arrived to relieve me for the graveyard shift.

When I left the hospital toward midnight, there was a teenage girl in new blue denim jeans and a powder-blue top standing beneath the neon sign outside. She had a pretty face, light skin, and the dirty-blond hair of a true rubiecita. Our eyes met and she walked over to me. Casually overlooking the mark on my cheek, she handed me a sack. "It looked like you were never going to get a break, so I brought you something."

Inside the sack was a malted milk and a sandwich. "Where did you get this?"

"At the Habana Libre cafeteria."

"They let you in?"

"A friend picked it up for me, a foreigner."

"Thank you. Let me pay you."

"I won't take your money, doctor. That girl you operated on tonight is my closest cousin."

"Please, share this with me."

"No thanks. I already ate."

I bit into the sandwich: ham and cheese on bread that wasn't stale.

"You're a lifesaver. I haven't tasted anything in twelve hours."

We talked about the heat while I finished the sandwich and the malta. Then she looked me in the eyes and said, "Pardon me, doctor, but a girlfriend told me you have a clinic where you can do the HIV test and keep the results secret."

I looked over my shoulder—nobody. "Yes, but when it's necessary I recommend treatment and counseling."

"I'm not going to one of those sanitoriums."

"You're getting ahead of yourself. My polyclinic is on 12 y 23 in Vedado. There are open consultations this Saturday and Sunday from 8:00 to 5:00. I close for an hour at midday."

"I'll see you tomorrow then," she said. The girl walked off into the night.

* * *

Back at the attic, I flipped on the light and said to El Ché, "The sun through the French doors has been sucking the color from your face."

El Ché replied, "You look like hell yourself. Even if there's not much to eat, you should at least keep clean-shaven."

"I can't buy a razor anywhere. And who are you to talk, barbudo?"

"My beard is different. It's symbolic."

"I'll say: totemic."

I flipped on Radio Reloj. "*Economic aggression from North American reactionaries has not dampened the spirits of the volunteer brigades picking cucumbers in Varadero . . .*"

There are certain advantages to occupying the third floor, like fewer encounters with the CDR and other people of the street. It's quieter up en el tercer piso and cooler in the breezes from the Florida Straits, and although there are relocados downstairs, none trudge overhead. For the past few years, I have resigned myself to every six months seeing all that sustains me—the real value of my salary, my ration of food and coffee, my allowance of sex, and the square footage of the house I can call my own—cut in half. I have a galley kitchen where I make coffee (when there is coffee) and slice whatever scraps of vegetables I can find on the bolsa negra with a dull scalpel salvaged from the pediátrico. The bathroom is tiny with a toilet, a basin under an iron tap, and a shower three feet square. In the living room there's a braided rug where I throw my dirty work clothes, three walls of books, and a sofa where I sleep beneath a poster of El Ché. I got rid of the bed after Elena left. The saving grace of this attic—added during pre-revolutionary days less for the servant-occupant's enjoyment than to appease the façade of proportion at the time—is a pair of French doors that open onto a shallow balcony facing the sea: a living blue movie where imagination paints ninety-mile-away views of that most unobtainable peninsula. On good days I get up and put Beny Moré on my father's old tocadisco. I open the French doors and let the ships' whistles blow in from Havana Bay. On bad days I awaken too early, hours before dawn, and stay on the sofa with my eyes squeezed shut but getting none of sleep's reprieve.

I lit a cigarette, brand Popular: black tobacco packed in sweet rice paper, ten cents a pack on the ration card, but that's for just one pack a week, and everybody who smokes Populares craves at least a pack a day. Now two packs of Popular go for an American dollar on the black market, so nobody who gives up smoking ever surrenders his weekly ration. Most people I know who have recently quit did it so they can go on eating. Coffee can help the headaches, when there is coffee. I use the grounds four or five times, dehydrating them in the window between infusions and preserving them with a bit of plastic in the refrigerator. Then again, coffee can be the cause. Neurons become greedy for caffeine, and when abruptly there is no more caffeine they become confused and send messages to the pain center. Coffee can hurt or coffee can be a remedy. When I was interning thirty-hour triples, I could try to plow through the migraine, but lately the pain has been making me dizzy. There's no more aspirin or ibuprofen. I'd have to steal it from the pediátrico, and that would mean directly from the patients' provisions. I won't stoop that low. Not yet.

There was no coffee, not even tea, but as a psychosomatic tactic I got an empty cup from the kitchen and took imaginary sips. Sometimes it stems the migraine. Every day is pervaded by headaches. Hunger headaches, heat headaches, just missed the bus and have to wait four more hours for the next one headaches. Berliners on la tele chiseling chunks of concrete to sell to American collectors headaches. Desperation headaches. Headaches of locusts pealing invisibly from saw grass and palm, of shrill locusts flying smack into your eye and crunching under your feet. Headaches that make your jaw ache. Headaches that begin between midbrain and cerebellum and rise, pausing to rock the pons, and shudder back down the spinal cord through the medulla oblongata. Headaches that settle into one shoulder or the other. Headaches that make you vomit. Headaches that make music, their very own music, broadcasting on low-frequency radio waves that shake the bowels of passersby.

"¡Radio Reloj! Son las doce de la noche." I lit another cigarette and turned on la tele, thinking there might be something good on Cine de Medianoche. There was: Oliver Stone's Jota-éFe-Ka. But just as it was beginning—¡ñó! Otro apagón. Blackouts follow schedules as faithfully as the Friday-night features.

12 August 1979

"¡Qué calentico y rico está!" Aurora bounced me in the furrow of her glorious thighs, off-key harmonizing with the man mamboing down 23rd Street. "¡Ya no se puede pedir mas!" With her ebony-smooth skin and pendulous breasts, it was the housekeeper, Aurora, who was the light of my young life. Not Mamá. Mamá was downstairs in her room, shutters closed against the heat of the Havana afternoon. She stayed in bed for long periods of time, days sometimes. My father had left for Miami in '69, two months before I was born, and now it was my tenth birthday and Mamá was dying of cancer. Aurora would insist Mamá hug me like you would entreat a sick person to eat: "Un abrazo, señora, por favor . . ."

After school I had gone straight up to Aurora's attic to play with dominoes until that twilight hour when the peanut vendor breezed by. As soon as we heard the call come up from Calle 23—"Cacerita no te acuestes a dormir . . ." and by cacerita I knew he meant Aurorita; she was his little housekeep—Aurora scooped me up, shifted me to her hip, threw open the French doors, and lowered the line with a peso in the basket. She reeled the basket back in and Machado, my pet dog, stood on his hind legs. Aurora swatted him. "¡Mendigo!" She stuffed the hot nuts in the front pocket of my overalls.

"Aurita," I said, "what's the man singing about that's so hot and tasty?"

"Algo que tu tienes en los pantolones."

"¿Y qué es eso?"

Yanking the paper cone from my pocket, Aurora cried, "¡Maní!"

Aurora unraveled the cone and poured me two handfuls. It was hot. It was good. I knew what the man meant. You really didn't want to go to bed without a little something hot in your belly. That afternoon Mamá seemed to be feeling okay, so Aurora took the evening off. Mamá baked us a cake and we had the world all to ourselves.

After Mamá died, I developed a small hemorrhage beneath my right eye. Many photos and X-rays were taken. Dermatologists and neurosurgeons first diagnosed that, if the hematoma were to burst, I could suffer a massive and likely lethal stroke. I carried a time bomb in my head. Should they schedule surgery? Would it do any good, or would it just trigger the detonator? Although I was allowed to leave the hospital in a few days, I had to return daily for medical observation. After two months the doctors decided that the thrombus was benign. Although the only thing the lab-coats did was figure out to leave me alone, my case was considered a milestone for Socialist medicine, a great prognostic step. The chief pediatrician was flown to Gdansk and Stockholm and Mexico City for conference presentations, complete with slide projections. An intern pointed out that the macula was shaped a little like Havana on the map. The custodians of Communist health care came up with a term for my *infarctus incubatus*, indexed in medical textbooks throughout Cuba, China, East Germany, Russia, and Angola: *Havana Lunar*.

My grandmother Mamamá moved into the house, but she grieved so deeply for Mamá that I was left in Aurora's care. In this way things were not much different from before. I did not play with other children. I would look in the mirror, wondering why the mark shows up on one side of my nose in photos, the other in the glass. I worried that I didn't really know which side to hide from strangers. What most disturbed me about someone seeing it for the first time was not the steady stare, the curled lip, or the involuntary "¡Qué raro!" or "¡Qué asco!" It was the follow-up among those brazen enough to ask aloud: "How did you get that?"

Aurora would take me to Cemeterio Colón, the necropolis, to visit Mamá. We passed the monument to the firemen, dozens of them who perished in a great conflagration at the turn of the century. On each corner of the tomb, a stone mourner bowed her head. I tried to peer up under the shrouds at their eyes, but these statues were never given sight. We passed the tomb of La Milagrosa, and Aurora told me the story of this famous resident of the necropolis. The woman died delivering a stillborn child. They were buried together, the child's corpse laid to rest between the mother's legs as was the custom in the early part of the century. Years later, when the widower requested that his late wife be moved, the remains were exhumed and they found the infant skeleton cradled in the mother's arms. Pilgrims visit her grave every day, requesting her intercession in all kinds of family matters.

At the corner of H y 8 was Mamá. Going to the grave was therapeutic for me. It was a place to be left alone not only by the doctors but by all the strangers around the neighborhood or at school who had heard of my tragedy. Just by stepping into Cemeterio Colón I was inoculated against anyone coming up to me and saying *I'm sorry.* I closed my eyes and tried to picture Mamá's face. She wasn't so different in death from the months leading up to it, losing a fight with cancer and very depressed. Now that she was out of her suffering, I loved her more than ever. There were days, sometimes many in succession, when I wished she had taken me with her.

At school I was given the nickname "La Mancha." I developed a crush on a girl in my class but was too young to know what to do about it. She sat directly to my left, and I stole glances all day long. Her light blue eyes: such a beautiful rarity on this island. The girl's eyes were windows onto another place, somewhere remote from Cuba, somewhere altogether different from this world. During reading time I lifted my book to shield my face and gaze sideways at those arctic eyes while the teacher, an embittered Catholic widower, graded papers with Last Judgment gusto. I taught myself how to speed-read through *Edad de Oro.* If I scanned the basic gist of the issue in four or five minutes, I was ready to deflect the oral comprehension questions, and then I could spend a good quarter-hour getting lost in the girl's icy countries. That's the cold North where my father is, I told myself. I knew winters in Miami weren't icy, but there was a supermarket with a big machine that made a mountain of snow in the parking lot to entertain the children last Christmas, which is what the gusanos celebrate two weeks before Reyes Magos. Perhaps if I touched the girl's hand and looked into those eyes, I could travel there to the cold North.

"¡Manolo! ¿Qué te pasa con el cuello?" The teacher came right down our row and loomed over me like a malicious gargoyle. Suddenly subjected to my classmates' scrutiny, I didn't even have the presence to turn away. My fellow students, happy to be distracted from their tasks, began to chatter, and the girl turned to face me. She was annoyed, anxious to get back to her book. She was looking at me for the first time, and there was nothing special registering for her. It was utter indifference I was looking back at. The teacher pinched my cranium and rotated my flushed face toward the book. "Qué bonitos ojos tienes ¿no?" the teacher blurted. The entire class erupted in laughter, except for the girl with blue eyes. As punishment, the teacher made me switch desks with the boy seated in front of the blue-eyed girl. No longer was I just "La Mancha." Now I was also called "El Enamorado," and my beloved became "Ojitos Lindos."

Near the end of the school year I set myself the task of observing a ghost. When Aurora was asleep one night, I left the house for the place they lived: the necropolis. I boosted myself over the wall and snuck past the gargantuan arch, wherein the groundskeeper lay sleeping. The moon, at its brightest, burned my cheeks while I penetrated deep into the heart of the cemetery to the corner of H y 8. I sat cross-legged against the tomb of Mamá's neighbor, cracked where tree roots had pushed through, and waited for a ghost to show. The sharp spines of obelisks glowed against the night sky, and my accelerated heart rate made it impossible for me to sleep. Finally, toward morning, I lay on my side to rest.

I opened my eyes onto a deep blue dawn. A narrow column of light emerged from the earth. My body rigid with sleep paralysis, I couldn't move to make sense of the apparition. I stared at it for an unmeasurable moment and felt no fear or curiosity, just the serene indifference of a hypnotic. Mesmerized, I shut my eyes. They didn't open again until I was aroused by the sour notes of a funeral procession. The brightness was blinding. A figure stood above me, eclipsing the sun, and when I shaded my eyes I was astonished to see the living spirit of my own longing come to greet me: Ojitos Lindos. "What are you doing here?"

"My father," she said, with a jerk of the head in the direction of the funeral. "He's the one in the box." Her soft voice betrayed no emotion, only the indifference of a child before the drama of death. "What about you?"

I sat up and squinted at the sky. The sun had already risen above the tombs. I was embarrassed to admit I had been trying to see a ghost, so I said, "Visiting my mother." It occurred to me that my mother and her father were both ghosts. They were alike, Mamá and Ojitos Lindos's father. I stood up and flicked the straw from my hair. "I'm sorry I caused you such trouble in school."

"What do you mean?"

"They called you names."

"They called you names too." She looked hard at me. Burning, wishing I hadn't reminded her, I looked away. "Well, don't you want to see?" she said.

"See what?"

"My eyes." I looked up and Ojitos Lindos glared back at me. Nobody had ever looked at me in quite that way. She was not staring at the mark. She looked at me and saw me, the real me, not La Mancha. With the big blemish on my cheek, people rarely looked me in the eye, but here in the necropolis with Ojitos Lindos nothing came between. I gazed straight through the light blue of her eyes to the brightening sky behind. The color was the same. "I have to go," she said. "My mother will send my uncle searching for me."

When I returned to the house nobody asked where I had been. The block was buzzing with news of the occupation at the Peruvian embassy, and Aurora spent all day in front of the television. On Monday Ojitos Lindos wasn't in school. Vacations were nearing, and her mother had arranged for her to stay at home in Oriente during their time of mourning. In the weeks after the fiasco at the Peruvian embassy, the port of Mariel became choked with boats from Florida picking up gusanos. A wealthy cousin sought Aurora out and took her to Miami to prove something, perhaps just that he had become wealthy. At the end of the school year, a neighbor took me to the bus terminal, where I was packed off to Pinar del Río to spend the summer with my father's family.

1 August 1992

Weekends at the policlínico are always busy, but on that Saturday a patient brought me coffee at lunchtime and I was feeling a little better when the girl came by in the afternoon. Outside the pediátrico the day before, she had seemed too modestly dressed for a jinetera. Now she wore the characteristic short skirt, tight T-shirt, and platform sandals of the girls who walk the Malecón. She was bajita, a little bigger than petite, and gordita, which is not to say fat, but shapely.

I told her that HIV antibodies take anywhere between six weeks and six months to develop. "This test won't detect any exposure to the virus that might have occurred in the past three months."

"I'd say it's none of your business, but I don't want you to get the wrong idea about me: I've had a steady boyfriend for over a year."

I took her blood sample and attached a numerical label. "Hold on to this ticket; the number corresponds to your test."

"Can't you give me the answer now?"

"I have to take your sample to the lab at the pediatric hospital. But you can come back here to get the results after 5:30 on Monday. I live upstairs, the top buzzer."

"What will I owe you?"

"Nothing."

"Surely you're taking a risk by not reporting the results to the government."

"I'll keep it a secret if you will."

"It's a deal. And don't be so sure I won't owe you."

After closing up the clinic, the question was whether to spend my week's pay from the pediátrico on a liter of gasoline or on eight ounces of coffee. Gasoline is sold in liters gracias a los Rusos, y los Chinos turned rice into kilos, but los Cubanos will always think of café in pounds and ounces. It was the night of the annual pediátrico cocktail party at the director's home, so I opted for the liter of gas, anticipating a ride with Carlota. The station attendant tallied up my coins with the look of disgust I have come to take for granted among government workers, sitting behind empty mechanical cash registers in front of stockless shelves, taking monotonous orders for sugar water and stale congris at desultory cafeterias, their jobs served up to the humiliating doldrums of the Special Period.

Up in the attic there was water, so I took a shower with a sliver of camphor soap scraped from a drain at the pediátrico. Before I finished bathing, Beatrice yelled up from the second floor, "MaNOlo! ... TeLÉFono!" I went downstairs barefoot, dripping in a towel. Gasoline turned out to have been the wrong choice for my two hundred pesos. It was Carlota calling to tell me she had one of her headaches. "I won't be much fun tonight. Would you mind going for a ride another night, maybe tomorrow?" Carlota, too, was on a telefono del vecino, and so for decency would say no more.

"Of course not. No te preocupes. Que te mejores rápido." I handed the phone back to Beatrice, who was grinning maliciously, and climbed the stairs to my apartment, letting the towel slip to give her a good look at my culo. I sprawled on the sofa and considered the liter of gas, wishing I had gotten café instead. Just one pot brewed on a Friday afternoon can give me a buchito every three waking hours through Sunday. With a little coffee in my belly, I don't notice hunger as much. I might even manage to accomplish a few cosmetic jobs on the Lada. But now, with a bottle of gasoline and no place to go, Friday night was shaping up to be a long, hot migraine session sprawled on the sofa to the accompaniment of a sour stomach.

A shout came up from the street: "¡Oye, Mano!" I pulled on a pair of pants and opened the French doors to look down. On the back of his moped sat Yorki, my best friend since el pre-universitario. While I had gotten interested in medicine, Yorki burned up jet fuel for fútbol. He played such good soccer en el pre that they compared him with a famous striker from the Czech team. All over Havana people still call him El Checo. I'd become a hard-up doctor and Yorki a sex-obsessed dishwasher, but he makes more money reselling fish the neumaticos catch along the Malecón than I do doctoring. Yorki peered up at me over his designer sunglasses. "Want to go for a walk?"

Walking: the one thing everyone can afford in the Special Period. When I walk alone, some people, mostly children or rude adults, can't help staring and sometimes commenting on my mark. Although for the most part the people of Vedado know and respect me for running the clinic, walking out of my neighborhood always brings new strangers. Once a Japanese tourist took a photo right in my face. There are also the regulars with their superstitions. One wide-bottomed mama with a jet-black dye always calls her children inside when I am coming down the crumbling sidewalk. But Yorki makes such an exhibition of himself with his running commentary that it eclipses my lunar.

We trotted along the sea wall while Yorki cast piropos at women young and old, beautiful and ugly, Spandexed and army khakied. "If you cook the way you walk, mamasita, I'll lick the burnt rice from the bottom of the pot." I was hustling to keep up. Without slowing, Yorki turned and said, "Ayer me comí un sabroso jamón con queso," touching five fingers to his lips to show me just how good that ham and cheese was. At the stone jetty across from General Machado's statue, we came upon a crowd of jineteras—rubia, morena, mulata, prieta. Yorki cried, "¡Mira esas nalgas!" but these girls had priced themselves out of his market.

Coco taxis tumbled around the statue of Máximo Gomez. Tourists were taking pictures of the billboard of enraged Uncle Sam. The tracheotomy case in the cane hat was leaving live fish flapping on the seawall sidewalk to bait conscientious tourists, imparting a solicitous grunt through the hole in his throat. Across from la Oficina de Intereses, Yorki clapped his hands together to signal joke-telling mode.

"Pepito walks in on his mother in the bath one day. 'Mami, what's that?' 'This?' she says, covering up. 'It's just . . . *whatever*.' Later some guests arrive and Pepito's mother asks if they'd like anything special for lunch, and the guests say, 'Oh, just make whatever.' Pepito hears this and pipes up, 'If we're having whatever for lunch, please do me a favor and pluck the little hairs from mine!'" Walking with Yorki is like walking around with a radio tuned, for once, to an interesting station, lively and perverse.

One of the jineteras on the Malecón recognized me from my basement clinic: "Oye, doctor, buy yourself some pants that fit you." She threw an American quarter at my feet, and I didn't get to decide whether or not I had too much pride to pick it up before a ratón del Malecón—a boy of seven or eight, shirtless in Chinese tenis—scrambled out of nowhere to scoop up the shiny limosna and hopped over the sea wall to the rocks ten feet below.

Yorki called over his shoulder to the teenage streetwalkers, "I'll be back later in case any of you delicious pastries doesn't get a date!" He said to me, "Nunca me casaré. If only to keep a clean license to grab a pair of nalgas como esas now and then. You'll never get married either, Mano."

"Except for when I already was."

"¿Quién? ¿Elena? That one doesn't count. That woman was a lesbian, but I could have converted her. ¡Cuidado con los tarros!" I ducked my head just in time to avoid catching my horns on a *Solo Ciclos* sign. Yorki's mission was to keep me on my toes and out of a second slip into the marriage trap. His philosophy: "Life, like the second half of a game of fútbol, is too short. Score often and from a variety of positions. And when the goalie leaves you a gimme at the net—by all means, brother, shoot!"

We made the better half of the Malecón—from 1836 to Paseo del Prado—in ninety minutes. Between Perseverancia and Campanario, Yorki hopped down to the rocks and peered over the top of his sunglasses to see what the divers had caught. They held up two small lobsters. Yorki whipped out a couple of bills, and the divers, flashing their knives, cut the tails off and gave him the bodies. "Coge." Yorki handed me the clipped lobsters, half-dead and writhing. He had trouble boosting himself back up the wall. Yorki is no longer the muscular teenager who can charge kids twice his size and rocket the ball into the net while the goalie dives in the wrong direction. Havana has lost a lot of weight over the past year and a half, and Yorki, clawing at the stone ledge, was stubborn and hungry like the rest. Gasping for breath he took the lobsters. "Those tails would have cost me la pinga."

"Are you going to sell these?"

"They're for me and my date."

"Who's the lucky lady who gets to try your famous sopa de langosta this time?"

Yorki, scanning the horizon through his shades, ignored this. The first time Yorki prepared a romantic dinner with lobster, he had to jump up shortly after dragging the girl to bed, the bisque coming out both ends.

"Remember to take out la tripa this time."

We walked back to Vedado and Yorki took off on the moped with his prize. I headed over to Cine Chaplin and snuck in through the broken door from the alley. After killing a little time napping through the second half of a bad ICAIC film on its third run, I walked to Centro Habana to flip through dusty old Egrem recordings at the music market before heading to the pediátrico coctail party.

In the penthouse apartment of a modern building on Avenida de los Presidentes, Director González greeted me at the elevator that opens onto his foyer. "Rodriguez, why didn't you bring a date?"

"I'm separated."

"I know. But I thought for sure you'd have a girlfriend by now." I was the first to arrive, so the director asked me to go down and buy some cigarettes. "Marlboro, por cierto. Four packs at the Riviera. Don't worry about the concierge. You look Criollo enough that he'll think you're a Spanish tourist. The tobacconist is through the doors and to the right."

I returned with the smokes and a dollar change. Director González said, "Keep the dollar,

Rodriguez—cómprate un café mas tarde. ¿Quieres un cigarro?"

"Gracias, pero yo fumo negros." I pulled out my own cigarettes and my father's silver lighter, lighting first the director's Marlboro and then my own Popular.

"¡Qué mal huelen!" the director said, frowning at my pack of Populares.

Colleagues began arriving with husbands and wives. The promised refreshments were brought out, and we guests checked ourselves to keep from looking too hungry while getting our share of the humble spread of salami sandwiches and Havana Club con Tropicola. The party was full of sycophants after a promotion, but late in the evening, over cigarettes and Mexican brandy, Director González pulled me aside.

"I'd like you to consider transferring to Sancti Spíritus, Rodriguez. The Revolution can market you. You're young and handsome, for a doctor. Madres españolas would pay ten times your current salary for you to take care of their little hypochondriacs, fix a few hairlips."

"No gracias, señor. I prefer practicing at the pediátrico."

"Very funny, Rodriguez. You don't have to kiss my ass, you know. You're Plan G."

The one opportunity for escape, available to

only a few physicians who, like me, are Plan G, is a job in medical tourism. Vacationing patients are the new pillar of the economy, replacing the Soviet sugar trade. I could leave crumbling Havana and live in a new condominium by the beach at Sancti Spíritus, but then I would have to practice at the health center for foreigners, pampering fat tourists with their penchant for prostitutes. I have gotten to know several pediatricians who cultivated Director González's favor and got transferred. They set up elaborate dialectics to ease their consciences: "Doctors can better serve the Revolution by hastening our assimilation into the modern, international economies . . ." But the Revolution educated our generation on a solid foundation of ideology. I didn't swallow all of it, but it was better than what motivates medical students in capitalist countries. Should we trade our principles for a condo on the beach, a light docket of consults, and an affair with a grateful mother or two?

"No, señor directór, I'd rather not go." There's a saying: *Que no van lejos los de alante si los de atrás corren bien.* Repeating this—*Don't go too much farther if the ones behind work harder*—has occasionally brought me into conflict with those in charge. Today I see medical tourism as a government machine like any other. El Comandante ulimately reaps the spoils of each physician's exploited specialty, making doctoring no different from the vocation of the reckless Panataxi driver or the indifferent waiter at the Habana Libre cafeteria, his left cuff caked with dried egg yolk.

Director González said, "If this has to do with getting passed over for South Africa last year, forget about it. That was regrettable. If I'd been on the committee, you never would have had any problem. The Revolution is much more integrated today. Talent is not wasted on account of a nuance of ideology. If you work hard and you work well, you'll get the promotions you deserve. The choice is yours, but if you ask me you're wasting your talent."

"Wasting it on the children of Cuba?"

"Noble response, Doctor Rodriguez. Let me put it this way: You're wasting the *Revolution's* talent. Anybody can fix a sprained wrist. But you have extraordinary gifts. The income you could generate for the Revolution would help many more Cubans—adult, elderly, and children."

"And the common people of Havana would end up swallowing the sacrifice."

"The pediátrico would find a replacement."

"Either an inferior intern or someone else who will eventually be invited to cross over. Besides, people in my neighborhood have come to depend on me at the clinic."

"There are other clinics. Vedado would get

along without you." Seeing me to the door, Director González said, "Take some chocolate, Rodriguez. It's Belgian, the best chocolate in the world."

"No, gracias. I'm allergic to chocolate."

"¡Qué raro! Y desafortunado . . ." Director González made me take the chocolate anyway, as well as a little leftover salami and a half-bottle of wine. "For a girlfriend. You should get yourself another lady, Rodriguez. You can imagine how parties like these, a little bit of rum and some sandwiches, are useful for heating up a courtship. They have a staff party every month at the institute in Sancti Spíritus. You could probably land yourself a rubiecita, if whites are what you like."

I walked up La Rampa, where only turistaxis sped by at that hour. There was a foot-cop on every block, but I walked with enough purpose not to arouse their sixth sense of paranoia. I was so hungry I could have eaten the salami there on the sidewalk, but I didn't, because I did have another lady now, didn't I? I couldn't fool myself anymore about Carlota being a creature comfort in the aftermath of Elena.

At the top of La Rampa, I remembered that there was a dollar in my pocket, so I headed to the Habana Libre to buy myself a café, a strong black one so that I could stave off the headache. I used to drink café the night before medical exams, and I aced most of those with ease. Then why was I shaking on this night, as if convinced I was fated to flunk the latest test of just one question and the best-odds option of answer: yes or no?

I raised a finger for service. "Compañero." The waiter stood at a distance and glowered, looking from my lunar to my cheap Chinese tennis shoes. I was not supposed to be in here. I was no longer his compañero. With his arrogant stare, the waiter impelled me out the door and back onto the street without my café.

I took the long way home on Carlos III, an avenue that has been darker than ever since the beginning of the Special Period. This is the spine of Havana, and inside a thousand shuttered houses from el Monumento de la Revolucíon all the way up to el Capitolio, the city was starving. She was sleeping, but it mitigated none of her hunger as she briefly dreamed, sometimes of pollos, lechones, tortas, empanadas, sometimes of adventures in America, sometimes of her own hunger. She would awaken to the same privations, each day collapsing into a heap of unnumbered others of scarcity and emptiness, and there was no practical guess at how many more would have to drop on this pile before she starved to death or was otherwise redeemed.

I walked past the pediátrico. The neon sign outside admitting reads:

VALE, PERO MILLONES DE VECES MAS, LA VIDA DE
UN SOLO SER HUMANO QUE TODAS LAS PROPRIE-
DADES DEL HOMBRE MÁS RICO DE LA TIERRA.

El Ché's quotation, burning like that on the wall
of the hospital, was dated before the workers even
flipped the switch. Now half the neon is out, and
doctors joke that it really reads:

THE TALENT OF A SINGLE JINETERA IS WORTH A
MILLION TIMES MORE THAN ALL THE POOR DOC-
TORS OF HAVANA.

2 August 1992

On Sunday afternoon I closed up the clinic and put the liter of gas in the Lada to drive out to Carlota's. It was Pablo's birthday and Carlota intercepted me at the curb. "Tell him we're going for a little birthday drive pa' tomar aire, then let me duck into Tío Tirso's on a pretense." Carlota told me there was a rumor going around Marianao of bread—fluffy white flour rolls, not tough pan integral, and fresh, made the day before. But she didn't want to disappoint Pablito. We would keep it a suprise in case the lead turned out to be false, or if they were just the usual sawdust-textured cakes made of harina integral.

Pablo climbed in back and I told him, "Feliz cumpleaños, viejo."

We cruised across Puente de la Lisa over the trash-strewn riverbed, where ancient trees born before José Martí breathe new oxygen on the breeze. I pulled up at Tirso's and Carlota climbed out with an armful of magazines and her awful poker face. "I'll just be a minute. I'm loaning Manuela some old Mexican *TV Guides* to reread."

"¿Qué pasa aquí?" Pablito protested from the backseat, only six but already wise to a woman's engaño. "Why is my mother acting so strangely?"

"It takes two hands to count your age now. You figure it out."

Eyes twinkling, Pablo said, "I could use toes too."

A minute later Carlota emerged with a grin on her face and her bag bulging, but she wanted to keep it a surprise a little longer. "Let's make it a short drive. How about we turn around at the edge of La Coronela?"

Pablo cried, "Oh, that's no birthday drive at all!"

"I know, but I forgot to turn off the water and Tirso and Manuela are coming over."

"¿Por qué?"

"Because I brought them the wrong magazines."

Pablo said, "Algo muy raro está pasando aquí."

Back at the house, Carlota bustled in the kitchen. She had managed to get some cheese and, together with the bread and the salami española that Director González had let me take home from his cocktail party, that meant real bocadillos. Manuela arrived and helped lay it all out in the comedor. I distracted Pablito on the solarium by blowing up surgical gloves into five-fingered balloons.

When the sandwiches were ready, Carlota called, "Pablo, ven para tu congrís." Rice and beans. He pretended not to hear. Pablito was past complaining.

"¿No oíste?" I said.

Pablo ignored the question. "Show me how to make a knot so the air doesn't escape."

"¡Pablo, ven! ¡Pab-LO!"

Pablo went into the dining room and saw what was really for lunch. "¡Mami! ¡Pan!"

"¡Feliz cumpleaños!"

Pablo was ecstatic: bread for his birthday. But it was like a bad movie on El Cine de las Ocho when Tirso rushed in seconds before we could sink our teeth into those beautiful sandwiches. "¡No! ¡Echaron vidrios en la harina!" I slapped Pablo's hand before the sandwich could get to his lips. Pablo saw real fear in my eyes and began to cry.

"Please, Pablito. There might be glass in the bread. There are bad people out there."

Tirso said, "The government did it to sabotage the black market."

Biting his lower lip, Pablo proposed, "We can try it, and if we feel something in our mouths we can spit it out."

"You don't feel it, Pablito. And it's not your mouth you have to worry about." I tied the bread in a plastic sack and put it in a metal trash can to keep the dogs from getting at it. We rinsed off the crumbs and rationed the salami and cheese in silence.

3 August 1992

At the beginning of my Monday shift I stopped by the lab to drop off the jinetera's blood sample. When I picked up the report at the end of the day, I was relieved to see that the results were negative.

Back at the attic El Ché complained of his nephew, who had been profiled in an enemy magazine for playing in a rock 'n' roll band that criticizes the Revolution. In the photo, the young Guevara had pasted a dollar bill on the front of his guitar. "¡Descarado! I appreciate his spunk, but did he have to blow it on a cheap pander to the Americans by prostituting himself to the *Time* photographer? If I were around I'd break that guitar in half."

"If I ever bump into him, I'll do it for you." There was a buzz from down in front and I opened the French doors. The jinetera looked up from the sidewalk. "Hold on." I came inside and got the spare key.

"Who's that?" El Ché asked.

"You'll see soon enough." I went back out on the balcony and dropped the key.

The girl climbed the stairs to the attic and sat on the small sofa. "You live here all alone?"

"Sí."

"What business does a man have living alone with such a beautiful balcony?"

"Do you find it counterrevolutionary?"

She gave me a sly smile. "I find it misogynist. You are depriving some good woman of a lovely view." Fidgeting, she gestured at the table. "Is this your examining slab?"

"It's just a coffee table. A sad joke, as there's no coffee." I sat beside her. "I have good news: The test was negative."

"I knew it." She reached for her purse and took out a box of Marlboros—empty. "Will you give me a cigarette?"

She pulled a Popular from my pack and I lit it for her. "I don't recommend becoming a regular smoker— for what it's worth."

"Very little." She exhaled in my face. Her eyes remained riveted to mine. "Let me ask you this, doctor: Are you a man?"

"Of course."

"Do you find me attractive?"

"You're a lovely girl."

"If you find me attractive and you're a man, why don't you sleep with me? What's keeping you? It could be a lot of fun."

"That's not the way I do things."

"How do you do things?"

"I wait until girls have had their quince, at least."

"That includes me. I'm sixteen."

"I don't even know your name."

"But now you know I'm clean."

"And it's up to you to stay that way." I stood up. "You'll have to pardon me, but I need to meet someone. Good luck, and please keep discreet about the testing at my clinic."

"Buenas noches, doctor."

When the girl was gone I lit a cigarette. El Ché annotated, "So, doctor, this is how you serve the Revolution, by taking in jineteras for private practice?"

"¡Cállate la boca!"

"Why are you bringing trouble into our home?"

That night Carlota left Pablo with Tirso and Manuela, and I took her to a paladar in Vedado. There was food for a change, more than just rice and beans: collard greens, with the tiniest bits of pork. Afterwards we parked at the docks and took the passenger ferry to Morro Castle. We made a picnic inside a giant magnolia with a half-full bottle of Mexican brandy left behind in the bush by a tourist. There was condensation at the top of the bottle, and the warm liquor had fermented a little extra in the heat and sun. A used rubber dangled from a branch, but I flicked it off with the end of a stick before Carlota could see it. We swigged straight from the bottle. "Nuestro vino es agrio," I told Carlota, "pero es nuestro vino." We were both empty-stomached enough that it was less than three minutes before we were giddy and flushed with the effect.

"Carlota, why do you go out with me?"

"¡Ai, Mano! We're here. We have wine. We're having a good time. Don't get philosophical."

"Why do you like having sex with me? I guess that's what I mean."

"That's easy. You're good."

"¿Y qué—?"

"Narciso! You want to know what makes you good? I'll tell you. It's not the thickness of the thing. A lot of men, at least Cubanos, got that."

"Carlota, no seas caprichosa."

"Well, it's true. What sets you apart is that you wait. And you wait and wait and wait. It's very considerate for a man."

"It's more fun."

"Well, most guys don't. Or they can't."

"Are you ever worried we'll fall in love?"

"I assure you: I love you only for your body—" Suddenly a bright flash and an explosion. "¡Dios mío! ¿Qué coño fué eso?" The distant patter of applause alerted us: el cañonazo de las nueve; every night at 9:00, a dozen Havanatur flunkies don colonial garb and shoot a blank cannon charge.

Back at the attic Carlota and I were settling into a smoke when Beatrice called up the stairs, "¡Manolo! ¡Teléfono!"

¡Coño! Who could it be?" I left Carlota fuming on the sofa.

Beatrice was in curlers and a housecoat, arms crossed on the landing. "It's a woman, a girl more likely. She already called twice while you were out."

I took the phone. "¿Qué hay?"

"It's me." The connection was crackly, but I knew who it was. "Can I come over?"

"Right now?"

"I need to go somewhere."

A clear, cruel misgiving made me blurt, "Not with a man, I hope."

"No, sinvergüenza. I'm alone, but I don't feel safe."

"I'm going to have to step out for a while."

"I don't care if you'll be there or not. I just need somewhere to go."

"Okay. I'll leave the spare key under the mat." I hung up and left Beatrice shaking her head. Back upstairs I told Carlota, "Let's go for a walk by the river."

"Bien," Carlota said with a sour note that belied a canny, feminine clairvoyance.

El Rio Almendares runs polluted as a sewage pipe, but it's the coolest place in the neighborhood. I sat on a stump and lit a cigarette. "I have a patient who is coming by the house in a little while."

"¿Y?"

"Y . . . es jinetera."

Carlota's voice went throaty: "Now you're going around with jineteras?"

"Just one jinetera."

"What does this have to do with me? We've always had an understanding that this isn't about love or marriage. Do whatever you want, but why kick me out of your apartment? That's not normal."

"No sé, Carlota, no sé . . ."

"You know what your problem is, Mano?"

"No sé."

"I'll tell you, even though it might not be a good idea. Do you want to know?"

"I want you to tell me."

"Then I'll tell you. Your problem is that even *you* don't know what you want."

"I'm sorry, Carlota."

She shook her head. "No. I shouldn't have told you. I shouldn't have told you anything."

"Let me drive you home."

"I can take care of myself. There's a girl who needs you. Go be with her."

Up in the attic the jinetera sat on the sofa, the spare key on the table. Her cheeks were tear-streaked, and the skin was red and swollen around her eyes. "I'm sorry to bother you like this, doctor."

I sat in the rocking chair and lit a cigarette. "¿Qué te pasó?"

"Alejandro is angry."

"Who?"

"My boyfriend. He's jealous."

"Jealous of what?"

"Of us."

"What do you mean? What did you tell him?"

"That I'm falling for you."

"Look, you stay up here tonight if you'd like. I'm going down to sleep in the basement."

"Doctor," she looked at me with piercing dark eyes, "you are denying your heart."

"Don't be so sure."

I went down to the clinic and stretched out on a cot. I hadn't slept down here since near the end with Elena.

12 August 1989

On my twentieth birthday I posed on the steps of el Capitolio, a forced grin frozen on my face. "Do you want me to superimpose the dome in the background?" the photographer asked.

"What do you mean?"

"This lens takes a good headshot, but otherwise only the steps of the Capitol show up. I can add the dome in the printing process."

"No. Just the portrait."

"Not even *Recuerdo de Cuba*?"

"I'm not a tourist. I was born here."

"Why didn't you say so? Special price for you. Two prints for ten pesos."

"One will be fine." Unlike the clinical photographers I had known in my youth who only wanted close-ups of the blemish beneath my right eye, this one touched tobacco-stained fingertips under my chin, giving it a forty-five-degree turn to the right to hide the mark. I turned back. "No. She would want it to show."

"For your lady?"

"Yes."

"Five pesos then. And you can keep the reverse-positive."

In the reverse-positive, my lunar showed up white like a crescent moon. Elena framed it side-by-side with the print and hung them above her vanity, the dark and light sides of me.

After I had started dating Elena, I told Carlota— who always said that she and I were "a sex thing"— no more sex. Elena and I made it through medical school together and both graduated Plan G. It's a little preposterous that they tell you G stands for genius. When the faculty nominated both of us for a four-year residency program in South Africa, Elena was happier than I had ever seen her. There would be English instruction as well as training in cutting-edge technology and techniques. We would be salaried while abroad. Anticipation for the adventure sparked her passion, and for the next few months I had the feeling that the residencies in South Africa might pull us through, be our escape.

In the fall I married Elena at the Palacio and we were given a cake and a voucher for a hotel in

Varadero. We watched the Wall go down on the television in our room—Berliners chiseling chunks of concrete to sell to American collectors . . . and everything that image carried in its wake. "*Compañeros, señores y señoras, this lapse in Eastern Europe affirms the need for Latin Americans to continue the fight against imperialism . . .*"

"What does this mean?" Elena asked.

"Capitalism has won."

"Won what?"

"*We shall stay on the road of Socialism with the help of our Soviet comrades. Hasta la victoria siempre. ¡Venceremos!*"

But all attempts at sterilization by all the propagandists at the Instituto Cubano de Radio y Televisión couldn't stop the spread of this virus. It would be a slow death. Over the next eighteen months, we watched as the Soviet Union collapsed and then COMECON dried up. First gasoline became scarce and the camellos started stinking up the streets with diesel. Then the blackouts began, up to eighteen hours some days. Then the meat and the cheese disappeared. By the summer of 1991 everything stopped. Fidel called it the Special Period. Nobody knew how long it would last or how bad it was going to get.

Before the final paperwork for Africa could be processed, the secretary of the Partido Comunista de

Cuba recalled my exit visa. Although I had been active in the Unión de Jóvenes Comunistas as a teenager, I had decided not to campaign for membership in the PCC when I realized how much indolence existed among the nucleus of the party. Now that the time had come to stamp my visa for South Africa, the secretary was taking his revenge. He cynically pretended indifference toward my nonaffiliation. Instead he alleged that my father's exile to the U.S. was grounds for concern about my possible desertion. Elena's visa arrived early, in the fall, although she wasn't scheduled to leave for South Africa until January.

I got depressed about the visa trouble, and Elena became distant and irritable. "I hear you speaking to that stupid poster," she said one day.

"He may be stupid, but don't call El Ché a poster."

"Will you please get rid of it? At least move it somewhere else. That's not the kind of thing that should be hanging in the middle of our living room. We're not del Comité."

"Believe me, I can't possibly move El Ché, y no te atreves tú."

"Why not?"

"Because there are no thumbtacks left." I knew she would ridicule me, so I told the truth only in my head: *Because it might break the spell. He might never speak to me again.* I believed this. I doubted I would hear El Ché very well if not for his charmed place-ment over the back of the sofa. Move just one of the tacks that hold his corners, just one inch, and next time I needed someone to talk to, El Ché would be mute.

Elena said, "What will you do while I'm gone?"

Raising my glass I said, "I will wait with the grape until you return."

"What if I never come back?"

I didn't answer. I didn't want to get into a fight. That would have meant definitely no sex later. Read-ing my thoughts, El Ché said, "It's already probably no sex."

After dinner I sat on the edge of the bed looking at my wife. Elena lay naked on the bedspread. She was almost asleep. She should have been under the covers. I moved to touch her.

"I'm tired, Mano."

"Yes, you're always tired."

"What's that supposed to mean?"

"I'm talking about the problem."

"There's no problem. You talking about it *is* the problem. You could start by just gently kissing my neck. Why don't you rub my shoulders or caress my back?"

"Just so you can fall asleep?"

"Well, if I fall asleep you can do whatever you want." Her eyes may not have betrayed the slightest glimmer of malice, but the air above her head was black with a greater menace: no-sex equals death.

Elena was in the final training course for South Africa when Carlota called. "How have you been, Mano?"

"Bien. ¿Y tú?"

"Bien. How are things with Elena?"

"Fine." Something about Carlota's call made me believe she was clairvoyant. Of course things weren't fine. I had made a mistake, many mistakes. I wanted to back up. I wondered whether I could regain my spark. "How are you?"

"My stupid cat's stuck up the stupid tree . . . again."

It took less than a second for me to go from feeling like a loser to feeling like a hunter. "Do you need a hand?"

"Don't bother, Mano. I can get someone around here to help me."

"It's no bother. I was just heading out to the pediátrico. I can stop by on the way."

"If you feel like it."

"I'll be there in about an hour, okay?"

"That depends on the buses."

"Not for me. I walk these days."

"Wow. They must give doctors better shoes than those Chinese rat traps the state stores are calling sandals."

"See you in an hour. Don't let that cat fall."

I dressed in a hurry. My hands shook so bad I had trouble with the buttons of my shirt. The nerves were not because I believed Elena might find out. It was excitement for Carlota, an arousal and suspense that I hadn't experienced since school days.

I spotted the cat about twelve meters up. She was perched like a loaf of bread near the end of one of the branches, waiting for it to grow below her and bridge the two meters of air between her paws and the high windowsill. She might have been able to survive the fall, but it would have left a man pretty messed up. I rang the third floor and Carlota came down. "What's up, Mano?"

"Hello, Carlota." I resisted the reflex to say, "You look nice." In a loose pullover and drooping jeans, she might not have looked nice to most men, but I knew what was in those pants. Just the shape of her skull made me want to run my fingers through her mousy brown hair. But first I would have to remove her glasses, the same wire-rimmed pair that always framed her cowish brown eyes. "I saw the cat."

"It looks bad, doesn't it?"

"It won't be a simple grab. Has she been up there long?"

"I get up this morning and feed her in the kitchen.

This afternoon I look out the window and see her floating there, looking in at me."

I started to climb, but the middle branches of the mimosa got too wobbly and I had to give up before getting halfway. "We'll have to bait her down somehow."

Carlota cooed, whistled, and blew kisses, but the cat didn't even look down. "She's cycloptic," Carlota said. "This is going to take some strategizing. Do you have time for coffee?"

"You have coffee?"

We went upstairs. The apartment was crowded with the deco collections Carlota has hoarded ever since she was a girl: cameo ashtrays, Bakolite dishes, monogrammed swizzle sticks. We sat across from each other at the kitchen table ignoring the cat, who was out the window and just out of reach. The coffee was hot and good. Carlota's skin, light for a Criolla, showed dark circles under her eyes.

"How's Pablo?"

"He's fine, at school. Do you want a little something to eat? How about a glass of milk?"

"You have milk?"

"Pablo's ration."

We took the center leaf from the kitchen table and extended it out the window with a little dish of Pablo's milk. The cat stepped right on. I pulled the board back in. "Isn't this how we got her down last time?"

Carlota smiled, disappeared into her bedroom, and emerged with her magic box. It was small and made of hardwood, with a hinged lid that had a hand-painted scene of Indian lovers kneeling on a rug and staring into each other's eyes, the woman handing the man a cup. "Shall we celebrate?"

I joined Carlota on silk cushions in front of her shrine to Santa Bárbara. She took her time pinching a Popular with a rolling motion, squeezing the tobacco out onto a copy of *Acuario*. Then she opened the top of her box, and a bouquet of marijuana filled the air between us. Carlota crushed the end off the bud and blended half Popular tobacco, half maní in the little machine from Holland. She always saved tampon wrappers for rolling papers. A perfect cigarette popped out. Carlota produced a pack of matches and paused before striking.

"If you're on the way to the pediátrico, you shouldn't—¿no?"

I grinned weakly—weariness mixed with the intoxication of anticipation. "I wasn't on my way anywhere. I'm on vacation."

I scissored the spliff between the index and middle fingers of my right hand. Carlota held the lit match while I puffed. Deep inhalation. Hold. I leaned toward Carlota's lips and exhaled slowly. We had to make the most of each toke. Our first kiss in more than two years was conscripted by the passage of aromatic smoke from my lungs to hers. Our mouths lingered. What began as practical puff-passing in an instant became lascivious as she slipped her tongue between my lips and put her palm on my khakis. I reached with my left hand and ran my fingers through Carlota's hair, clutching her skull and pressing our faces closer together. I caressed down her cheek and over the front of her shirt—her nipples popped awake—then underneath to her abdomen, where I fingered the hernia scar that had anchored me to Carlota over months of fantasies. I plunged my fist between her legs to stroke her rhythmically through the denim. Then I looked down at the spliff in my hand. I breathed. Carlota smoothed her hair. A conciliatory mist rose as materially as the first puff. It was a good roach we still had to finish. I passed it to Carlota and we touched fingers. Carlota took a deep puff and put the smoldering roach in an ashtray. At the edge of the knit rug, the roach singed a knot of sheep's wool, conjuring an unpleasant and arousing incense.

It was a cool November night when I realized Elena had taken down the photos. Winter had come early. Anticipating a numbing dinner together with our mutual disenchantment—a malaise that had begun to take such definite shape in mind's eye that I set an imaginary place for it to my right—I uncorked the sticky seconds of a Chilean Cabernet that Director González had found not quite to his taste. Elena and I sat in brooding camaraderie through our paltry, home-prepared dinner: arroz con mango, just like the joke. It spooked Elena that, for the better part of our two years together, the whole country had been going to shit. She was scheduled to leave for Africa at the start of the new year.

"Elena, what happened to the photos?"

"What photos?"

"The ones of me you kept above your vanity."

"I loaned them to my palero."

"What for?" It was a casual question. I didn't know enough about Palo Monte yet to guess anything other than my wife might want to show her santero friend what her husband looks like.

Elena brimmed with chilly charm. "So that when I leave, you will never love anybody again."

Elena left in January and I began the residency at the pediátrico. At the beginning of the summer she gave it to me in a letter. I have to hand it to her: She broke it off cleanly. She wrote that she was in love with a local, happier than ever. I had too much pride to write back.

I took Elena's letter with me on the ferry, but I already knew the palero would tell me he couldn't help. Nevertheless, I had to make the journey. The boat docked in Regla and I asked after the right place. The old woman who begs in front of the church remembered Elena the moment I described her eyes. "¡Qué bonita era! ¿Es tu esposa?" When I mentioned the separation, the beggar frowned as if to say: *If your wife went to see the palero, it's already too late.* She pointed a bony finger to his rooftop. For good luck, I threw a five-peso coin on her plate. The old woman turned away.

"Buenos días. Soy—"

"I know who you are," the palero said. He was a muscular old prieto dressed in white. "Nothing supernatural, doctor. I've seen your picture, haven't I? Come in. Sit down." The palero told me he was a specialist in romantic revenge. We sat in his small solarium and he showed me the little shrine where he invested objects with spiritual powers. "The photograph is consecrated to a diety who uses the image as an index," he explained, "capturing a lover's spirit and rendering it a prisoner of the paper. Offerings of fruit, money, tobacco, and coffee nurture the image in its process of becoming a powerful idol. After a few days, the lover's destiny is completely absorbed in the material image, and the palero tenders the idol to the supplicant, who may do with it—and with the lover—as he or she pleases. In your case, the photographs have probably been hung upside-down somewhere: the prescription for holding captive someone's heart. I did tell her that the charm's power would be more effective if she hid the pictures near where the lover sleeps. But there is nothing I can do about it now. The job is out of my hands."

He stood up. I thanked him for his time and rose to go. At the door I lit a cigarette and hesitated.

The palero read my thoughts. "You don't owe me anything, compañero, but I'll give you one last piece of advice: You should get help from another palero. There is something very dark at play with you. This trabajo of mine is nothing by comparison."

Back in Vedado I looked for the photos in cluttered closets, taped to the backs of drawers, beneath the shelf paper inside the kitchen cabinets. No luck. Suspecting Beatrice's complicity, I waited until she was out and picked the primitive lock on her apartment. I took apart framed photos of her homely parents, sisters, neices and nephews. A few of the mattes were backed by smiling portraits of a man whose wickedness must have been obvious to all in the very narrowness of his mustache—obvious to all but Beatrice, at least for a time. I returned to my attic empty-handed. I thought about what Elena's palero did with those photos and wondered if I would ever love again.

4 August 1992

In the morning I took a walk down the alleys behind the Riviera and bought a bunch of bananas
for twenty pesos. When I returned to the attic the
girl was asleep on the sofa wearing just a white tank
top and a purple thong. The sheet was twisted down
around her legs. I bent over the pile of laundry to
pick out clean scrubs for the morning. Warm laven-
der radiated from her sleep and her blue eyelids fluttered. Reaching for the uniform, I lightly brushed
her wrist and my heart skipped a beat. From his perch
above the sofa, El Ché brooded: "¡Qué cogido!"

I took two bananas and left the rest for her on
the coffee table. I wished there was coffee, wished
there was more than bananas to eat. Congris would
almost have cut it, if there had more than two beans
to add to a cupful of rice.

When I got home after my shift I bumped into

Beatrice on the front step. I bowed my head and said, "Buenos días."

She blocked my way and picked in the nest of hair beneath her bandana for a small box of matches and a filterless Popular. "Do you mind if I smoke, doctor?"

"No, but I have to discourage it for the sake of your health."

"For my health?"

I answered on the party line. "It's been years since El Comandante quit smoking."

"What does it matter to you what El Comandante does?" She smiled around her cigarette. "You forfeited the party's injunction to join the directorate." Beatrice has a way of turning up one corner of her mouth when she spouts out doctrine picked up piecemeal and reassembled in her petty, paranoid head: this recent article in *Juventud Rebelde*, that obscure "Año de los Diez Millones de Toneladas" speech by Fidel, or another dusty Martí discourse from *La Edad de Oro*.

I had to crack a smile a little like hers. "M'importa todo. It matters to my job, my freedom, my Cuba."

"I have always known you to be resistant to integration, doctor, but I never expected this."

"Expected what?"

"Do we really have to tap dance around the ideological details?" She took a deep drag. "The young lady who stayed at your place last night is a known prostitute."

"What my patients do for money is none of my business." I nudged past Beatrice and climbed the stairs to the attic.

When I opened the door I heard the shower running. It was good to know there was water. "Aren't you going in there with her?" said El Ché. I ignored him, kicking off my shoes. There was a sharp knock at the door. I opened and was surprised to see not Beatrice but a young man, black, slick-groomed, dressed in pantalones cortos and new tenis Americanos.

"We need a doctor. The neighbors said there's a doctor who lives up here."

"I'm a doctor."

"It's him," the boy called down to the landing, and two more teenagers, one black and the other white, scrambled up the stairs. When all three were inside, the third boy—pale, thin, with effeminate movements—shut the door behind him. He was so underweight that his small, striped T-shirt bunched at his chest. His green eyes glowed with a cool hatred I had seen a number of times before among young men on the sea wall.

I said, "No tengo dinero."

"Relax, Hipócrates, we're not here for your money." I instantly understood what they had come for. El Ché's expression said, *I told you she'd be trouble.*

The boyfriend Alejandro said, "Where is she?"

"I'm here alone."

"That's her in the shower, right, doctor?"

The black boys began bouncing on the balls of their feet. They were true black, prietos, brothers—not twins, but only a year or two apart—each one's face with its own language of scars and lacerations. The younger one glared at me with a jealous hostility. The older, the more scarred, avoided my eyes, my face, perhaps recognizing our blemished kinship. Both brothers were pretty big for undernourished times.

Alejandro said, "Man, you sure are one ugly maricón. She told me about the spot on your face, but I didn't believe it could be so fucking big. Now I know why you became a doctor. It's the only way you can get into a girl's pants."

"The CDR captain for this block lives right downstairs," I said. "She's probably already calling la patrulla. Why don't you leave? You haven't even been here."

He looked me in the eyes and said, "I would so love to see you get cut up."

The girl stepped into the living room in my ratty brown bathrobe, the belt tied above her hips. "Get out of here," she hissed at him.

"You were supposed to be taking a little time off," said Alejandro. "The other girls have started talking."

"Fuck them."

"'¿Qué pasó con la rubia?' they whine. 'She abandoned us for that doctor of hers.' 'Does that little puta think she can be a nurse?'"

"What the girls say doesn't mean shit to me."

"But it matters to *me*. The other chulos get talking and it's not so nice: 'Trouble holding onto your putas? If you're going to survive you can't just let your investment walk away.'"

"¡Vete al carajo!"

Alejandro pouted like a girl. "I could imagine you coming to me and saying, 'I want out of this game.' I might accept that. But I haven't heard you say that."

"I'll say it: I want out."

"But now you're just saying it to spite me in front of this faggot. You don't really mean it."

"Leave me alone, hijo de puta! You're psychotic!"

"Psychotic? So now you're Doctora Jinetera? Did this ugly maricón teach you some Freud?"

I stepped between them. "Oye, compañero—"

"Go to hell, mariconcito!" he spat. Alejandro said softly to the girl, "Do you really not want to come back?"

"I don't. I hate it."

"Do you want more money?"

"¡Vete al carajo, bestia! ¡Vete de aquí!"

He crossed to the door and said to me, "She makes fun of you, you know."

The younger black brother hit me on the side of the head with a fist like a club. I went down on the braided rug and the brothers followed Alejandro out the door. He called from the landing, "Even the ones who pay for her have to give her back when they're finished."

The girl locked the door and got a wet towel for my head. "I'm so sorry, doctor."

"No te preocupes." After I got over being stunned, my head didn't hurt too much. I crawled over to the sofa. The sun went down and there was another blackout. The girl dug around in the cabinets by the light of the stove burners. She took out the old tins and pried off the lids to find a hardened block of sugar and enough stale flour to make bread with the bananas I had bought that morning. We pulled the sofa cushions to the floor and turned it into a candlelight picnic.

"Julia, doctor—that's my name," she told me. "It was my cursed luck he was at Coppelia that day. 'Do you want some ice cream?' Of course I did. He was so sweet that first week. If I had asked around, I might have found out I'd taken up with the most sadistic chulo en la Habana. But in the beginning the other jineteras were like sisters, and the work was kind of fun."

"So you would pick up men along Quinta Avenida after midnight for fun?"

"For fun, yes, and sometimes money. But I wasn't a prostitute. I was a jinetera. There's a difference. I didn't sleep with anyone I didn't want to, and I didn't set a price. That kind of business is a barbarity of capitalism."

"Jinetera socialista y revolucionaria. Interesantísimo."

"I appreciate your bedside manner, doctor . . . He started me out on the beach in Guanabo, and the first two times it wasn't bad—timid guys: a Spaniard, then a Swede. The Swede was funny because he couldn't speak any Spanish, but I understood what he wanted all right. After the Swede there was a cruel, tattooed Colombiano. Alejandro never weeds out the abusives. I only did it a few weeks, but some of the rougher chulos threaten the girls if they try to quit before paying back the investment. The police protect them, you know. They take Alejandro's bribes. He works for one of the higher-ups . . ."

When the migraine came and I wasn't able to keep my eyes open any longer, I found a sheet and a bundle of old scrubs for a pillow and fell asleep on the braided rug.

5 August 1992

On Wednesday I woke up with a post-concussion headache on top of the migraine. I left Julia asleep on the sofa and walked to the pediátrico. In the afternoon I got home from my shift and was on my way up to the attic when Beatrice handed me the phone. It was Cousin Emilio calling from Pinar del Rio.

"Hola, primo. How's the house? Is that embittered solterona on the second floor still crowing for your cock?" Emilio thought this was doubly funny because Beatrice, who had just handed me the phone, was probably eavesdropping at that very moment.

"Every night. But I prefer masturbating along to my Celia Cruz records."

"Are you coming out to the rancho this weekend?"

"Sí, primo."

"Oye, Mano, if everything works out, we'll have

ourselves a little boating excursion on Saturday. I'm scheduled for a solo patrol."

"I'm supposed to look forward to that? I get seasick on the Regla ferry!"

"I'll see you this weekend."

In the attic Julia made tea with leaves that she had found in the cupboard from Abuelo's garden in Pinar del Rio. We sat at the kitchen table drinking tea and ate the last of the banana bread.

"I have to go to visit my family in Pinar this weekend," I told her.

"Let me ask you something, Mano," she said. "Do you think a person can ever really change her life?"

"It's never easy, but yes. We have to hope so."

"If you change, do you leave what you were behind, or do you always carry it with you?"

"My grandfather says, 'Minds change long before lives.'"

"What I want to know is: Can a person leave an old life behind so that there's no stain?"

"I don't know. Sometimes a piece of your past doesn't want to let go."

"Guilt. Conscience."

"Or just memory. The replay of memory. Good memories turn sour with too much remembering."

"And bad memories?"

"They turn better, maybe."

"No. Not so far."

"Maybe there's always an echo, a residue. But you have to fight. Fill your life with something new."

She said, "I want to change. I want to figure out something good I can do, like you . . . Don't look at me like that! I know I'll never go to medical school, but I could be a teacher. I could take care of children and teach them things, the difference between right and wrong."

"I believe you could," I said, standing. "I'm going out for a while with a friend."

"A girlfriend?"

"No, just a friend. We walk the Malecón. Do you want to come?"

"I better not go there till things settle down with Alejandro."

Walking the Malecón cooled my juices and I told Yorki about Julia. "Why don't you sleep with the girl, Mano? Split that melon open from above! Lather up that beard! Stick it in her culo, if she'll let you. Hell, do it whether or not she lets you! She'll love it once it's in. ¡Tengo ganas de darte tremenda cabilla!" That last was for a brown-skinned girl in a very tight white T-shirt and a vinyl miniskirt with a split that went right up to her G-string. She chased after Yorki and he had to jump to dodge her, almost losing his sunglasses.

"You must be careful with those dirty mulatas. They always grab your balls."

When we got back to Vedado it was already dark and I opened the clinic to sleep on a cot.

6 August 1992

On Thursday I got home from my shift at the pediátrico and sat at the kitchen table to look at my medical journals. I was too distracted, really, to call it reading. Having Julia in the attic was reminding me of the last woman I lived with in this small apartment.

"I asked around the jineteras in Vedado," she said. "Why don't you ever sleep with any of the girls you test?"

"It's immoral to trade sex for money or services."

"It's like biting the bullet for you, isn't it, doctor, this moralistic discourse on sex?"

"What do you mean 'biting the bullet'?"

"¿Eres hombre, no? You want to sleep with me, but you don't dare."

"No. I don't want to sleep with you."

"What are you afraid of? Is it that you don't find

me attractive or that you really are a maricón?"

"I'm going down to sleep in the clinic."

I went downstairs but I didn't sleep. I was thinking of someone all the time, and it wasn't Julia, and that's what terrified me. I hated giving credence to this superstition of a curse, but something about my animus was sealed inside those photos. I couldn't blame Elena for taking them. I had given them to her.

On Friday after my shift I took my pay to the bolsa negra and picked up a bottle of chispe tren and some rice and beans. When I got back to the attic I packed an overnight bag for Pinar del Rio.

"If it's all right with you," Julia said, "I'll just stay here another day or two."

I wasn't sure how I felt about her staying, but I couldn't bring myself to tell her to leave. What was the point of this liason? A search for love? No. She was simply a remarkable girl. She seemed to be sharpening everything that had become dull and indifferentiable in the fog of lust that accompanied my relationship with Carlota.

I gave Julia the rice and beans. "There should be enough food here until I get back on Sunday. Keep the door bolted."

"Don't worry, Mano. Those punks won't come around again."

I drove through the Almendares tunnel to Miramar and out Quinta Avenida. Before getting on the Carretera Central, I pulled over and took Hernán out of the trunk. When the pediátrico upgraded to a synthetic skeleton last year, Hernán had so many broken bones that it wasn't worth holding onto him. Director González wanted to stay out of trouble with Palo Monte by giving him to someone trustworthy, so Hernán fell to me. The Lada's back windows are tinted, but the license plates are state. That means I have to stop if hailed by the yellow-shirts. When they see an empty seat, they pounce into the breakdown lane and flag you over. Even after making it past prominent stops like La Novia del Mediodía, there's always the chance that one of those vultures will spring out at any point along the highway from the shadow of a parasombra, throwing my happy solitude into a headlock. I didn't feel like being forced to pick up a hitchhiker, so I propped Hernán in the passenger seat wearing a hooded fútbol shirt and Mickey Mouse sunglasses. In case I should ever get pulled over, I keep a letter from the director in the glove compartment to prove Hernán's not stolen.

In the reservoir at the outskirts of Havana, neumáticos fish from floating inner tubes. You know you're getting into the provinces when the organ pipes of the sierra appear on the right-hand side of the horizon. On the median, bare-chested boys in tattered shorts hoist platters of guayaba con queso over their shoulders. Everyone slows, mulls it over: a fat slice of sweet guava and a wedge of homemade cheese for a few pesos. Pull off the road and they'll run a half-minute hundred meter with their ten-pound platters. I pulled over. The last boy raced up and showed his guayaba y queso. Before I was done dealing with this one, another kid ran up with a great braid of garlic over his head. I bought a little bit from each and pulled back on the highway, leaving them both gawking at famished Hernán.

At kilometer seventy-five the road began to curve directly into the setting sun. Estábamos en provincia. At the entrance to the city, I drove past the statue to los Hermanos Saíz, then through Pinar, and out to Viñales.

I didn't want to leave the Lada down at the mural prehistórico, where any unattended cars arouse suspicion when they close the gates at sunset, so I parked in town and put Hernán back in the trunk. A few trucks pulled up to offer rides, but I prefer to follow the road from town to the dark side of the valley on foot, three kilometers up a shadeless, steady slope. It helps me get in the right frame of mind. The poinsettias grow enormous on either side of the trail. Later in the summer, a river runs between these rocks and I can't climb this way without getting covered in mud. I passed over streams and between farms and started up the spine of Abuelo's mountain. Pinareños know how to make use of every part of the palma real. The bark becomes walls, the pencas and yaguas finish the roof and also make the best cigar boxes. Take the natural tint from the stones of the mogotes to paint bohíos or henhouses.

Abuelo sat in his chair in front of his wooden house. "I saw you coming an hour ago."

I kissed my grandfather's cheek. "You've got the eyes of an eagle, Abuelo." He is also named Manolo, although ever since becoming a grandfather, everyone, his own children included, has called him Abuelo. My uncle Manolito, who is a month older than me, was dubbed diminutively because, as Abuelo's son, he had been born to another Manolo. When I, the city boy, first visited Viñales in the summer of my tenth year, I was called Manolo to keep things easy for Abuela, although most of my father's family still calls me Mano.

Something smelled good. Going to Viñales, there's actually food. Guajiros always scrape something together. In the bohío Abuela and Lydia were already at work on lunch. I kissed them both and gave Lydia the garlic, Abuela the bit of guayaba con queso. They don't have Havana's metropolitan walks en provincia, but there's always a bit of pork and a garden supply of coffee. I thought about how much Julia would like it here.

I went back out to sit with Abuelo. "I brought you a little chocolate. It's Belgian, el mejor del mundo."

"You never forget about me, Mano."

Abuela brought us café and we watched a pair of hawks spin their sunset shadows into mesmeric lace on the mountain. They rose on the updrafts without a single flap of wing. When we heard the ox low from the valley trail, Abuelo said, "Viene Manolito." My uncle Manolito was coming up from the field. Wild Manolito can climb the mountains like a tiger. He believes that taking the trail is lazy if you don't have a mule or ox to mind, so wherever possible he goes right up the steepest rocks. I told Abuelo I would surprise Manolito and got up to hide with the hens.

My plan was to come jumping out of the hen-house just as my uncle arrived, but while Manolito tied up the ox at the edge of the vega he was already hollering, "¡What cabrón is hiding with my hens?" Manolito's dogs got to barking and I came skulking out with my bottle of Ron Mulata.

"How did you know, Tío?"

"Muy fácil . . . I *smelled* you." Manolito's whoop carried out across the valley and echoed off the mogotes, hysterical laughter that always reminds me where that phrase *reir a carcajadas* comes from: side-splitting, ear-splitting, tree-splitting laughter. They could probably hear him all the way in Havana.

My uncle and I shared a bear hug, Manolito almost crushing one of my ribs. Un grito: "¡Mono!" Monkey, he calls me.

He tied up the mule so she wouldn't eat green leaves and get too fat. "Mules will eat anything, just like goats: maíz, palmiches, hasta café." She drank from the same bucket he used to wash her hide. He said to her, "Drinking soapy water, that's what you like. Mira qué mujer es esa mula." Then Manolito sent up a shout: "¡Hay hambre!"

From the bohío Lydia called, "Ya está listo."

This eased my uncle's mind. There was still work to do, and we took a minute to give the chickens feed corn. Manolito broke hard kernels off the cob with the heel of his hand. He gave the husks and cobs to his pigs. "You've got such pretty hands, Mono, like a lady, but nothing except your belt to hold your pants up." Manolito himself has no belt, but his muscular hips hold his workpants on his ass even when he shimmies up the trunk of a royal palm.

We all crowded around a table to eat. Abuela is too old now to do the actual serving, but she refuses to eat until Abuelo is finished. It has always been this way, but she has slowed down, passing serving duties along to Manolito's wife now that the rest of her children have left. Abuela said, "Why do wives today have to talk and talk and talk so much at their husbands? He's the father of her children. She should serve him. What does talking and complaining accomplish? In sixty years of marriage, Abuelo has never had to hit me. Not once." Abuelo is peaceable at the head of his table. He inhabits a place perceptible only to nineteenth-century patriarchs. The universe, his universe, of nine children and, according to Abuela, between sixty-five and seventy grandchildren, really does revolve around him. He is at its locus, although many orbits, like my father's, have set off so wide that the arc is almost unrecognizable.

Abuela said, "Todavía no te has casado, Manolo?" She meant remarried.

"No."

"Don't you want to have children?"

"You got started young, Abuela."

"Y tu muy tarde, y todavía." Lydia cleared the plates and I lit a cigarette. Abuela frowned and placed coffee before me. Abuelo is almost fifteen years older than her. Watching Abuela sweep the patio, I considered how here in the countryside nobody thinks twice about the age difference.

After eating her own merienda in the kitchen, Lydia began work on la cena. I told her to put me to work, and Manolito came over to see what we were doing. "¿Qué coño estás haciendo aquí?"

"Separating the garbage from the rice."

"Leave it. That's woman's work."

Manolito spent a minute or two inside the pigpen sadistically teasing the fat young sucklings. *"¿Quién será la que me quiere a mi?"* Whenever I show up in Viñales, Manolito insists on killing a piglet. *"¿Quién será? ¿Quién será?"* He knew the one he wanted. He'd had his eye on her all month. But, glowering into their frightened eyes, he took a minute to rile them up, slapping asses and tweaking corkscrew tails. *"¿Quién será la que me dé su amor? ¿Quién será?"* He caught the fattest one, raised her face to his, planted a sloppy kiss on her snout, and yowled in her ear. *"¿Quién será? ¿Quién será? ¿Quién será? ¿Quién será?"* He dragged the squealing animal out of the pen and across the patio to the foot of a tree. The dogs barked ravenously in anticipation of their take. With the jerk of a lightbulb chain, he pulled the knife across her bristling throat. Her squeals ceased and the dogs leapt. Gutteral grunts grew softer as she drowned in her blood, the dogs lapping up the red mud. Manolito dragged the piglet to the bohío. When I strayed too close to the sow she lunged at the end of her rope. "¡Cuidado, Mono! That mama is a mean one."

Manolito sent my ten-year-old cousin to the neighbor's with an empty two-liter bottle for some wine—distilled from cane with a touch of guanábana for color. Manolito poured two glasses. I sipped slowly but he goaded me, prying my mouth open and tipping my chin back if he had to. He poured it right down my throat from the bottle, so by the end we had both drank about the same amount.

"Manolito, you spend the whole day working beneath this sun and then immediately start drinking this awful wine. Why don't you rest a bit?"

"That's what I'm doing, Mono: resting. That's why we're drinking."

"What I mean is, why don't you rest a bit from the drinking?"

"What do you think I am, Mono, a vagrant? If I fall asleep after a hard day of work, I won't have time to drink before it's tomorrow already and I have to go back to work. I'm a man. I've got three duties: to work, to drink, and to fuck."

When the roast was ready, Manolito gave me the first taste. "Isn't this the most succulent little piggy you've tried in your life?"

"It's delicious."

"I feed them all coconut husks. The sow's milk is sweet enough for you or me to drink."

Manolito stumbled off to his bohío, and soon my cousin Emilio arrived in his coast guard uniform. After he had showered and put on clean clothes, Emilio pulled two chairs out onto the patio and produced a small bag of marijuana. He crumbled up a bud and fashioned a big twist with a square torn from a brown paper sack. "Where do you get this stuff?" I asked. He smiled but didn't answer. We smoked. We could hear Manolito and Lydia yelling at each other in the bohío. "Such an unhappy marriage," I said.

"That's redundant, Manolo. *All* marriages are unhappy."

"What about Abuelo y Abuela?"

"They don't count."

"Why not?"

"They're from another time."

I thought about what Emilio said and realized that there's no way to explain what actually makes me shack up with someone. It hasn't happened with enough women for me to identify a common quality. Something in the eyes contributes to it, but something different every time. In Elena it was that pure clarity. In Carlota it was smoldering lust. And Julia? She simply wanted to sleep with me, and it showed in her eyes. Why me? Maybe she had a little bet with her friends that she could get me. Good for her. Maybe she had a thing for my lunar. I should let myself enjoy this teenage girl, ¿no?—a reformed, or at least reforming, sex worker who wanted nothing more than to entertain me up in my little crow's nest above this Socialist island adrift. I knew that one way or another, if I let her get her hooks in me, all I would want is to press our bellies together—again and again.

12 August 1980

When I first came to Pinar del Rio at age eleven, I was in awe of what a different world existed on this island. All I had known before was Havana, a crumbling city of stone like a necropolis for the living. In Viñales all was green, and sugarloaf mountains hulked around the valley like slumbering elephants, sheltering the soil of tobacco country.

My cousin Emilio met the bus where it let me off at the mural prehistórico, and we wound our way between the rows of tobacco plants across the valley and up the side of our grandfather's mountain. At the top, Abuelo sat in his chair in front of his house. "I saw you coming an hour ago."

I kissed his cheek. "Tienes los ojos de águila, Abuelo."

Abuela emerged from the bohío and pressed me to her breast. "Pobre Manolo, tu mamá en el cielo y tu papá mas lejos que eso." When Abuela said my father was further away than heaven, she meant Miami.

Together with my uncles, aunts, and cousins, our number breached a dozen, but somehow Abuela managed to seat the entire family in two shifts and feed us all in under an hour. Abuelo had made the table out of the remains of one of the last trees he had cut for the walls of the bohío.

For the first serving with his eldest sons, Abuelo sat at the head, where one leg was a little shorter than the rest. Abuelo kept it this way because if he had to make a point, one thump of his rock fist served to upset every dish down the entire length.

During the second sitting, a stray pea or garbanzo rolled off someone else's plate and into my domain. The instant I shoved the legume into my mouth, Manolito hollered, "¡Pendejo, Mano! ¡Ese era mi frijol mágico!" Unfazed, I gobbled up the tidbit. Manolito then expanded on his patent outburst with sadistic little remarks like, "Todo el día mientras sudaba en la cosecha, guardaba ese frijolito aquí en mi culito." My cousins shrieked with glee and collapsed all over each other, troubling the tippy table with volcanic tremors. Abuela whacked the back of Manolito's skull with a serving spoon. "¡No seas sucio!"

Abuelo typically ignored Manolito's comments on my lunar, but when he heard Manolito say that I probably wouldn't be wanting cake on my birthday, Abuelo turned savage, lunging halfway down the length of the table and hammering his youngest son with a closed fist, cutting off the customary hyperactivity and leaving all the cousins sullen.

My first girlfriend was a Pinareña that first summer in Viñales. She lived in town. I don't remember her name or how we met. She said I could come over at 9 o'clock and watch the novela on TV.

On my way back to her house, I stuck to the shoulder of the unpaved road, popping coffee beans in my mouth, cracking them between molars to release their oil and essence. It was gritty. The taste was wicked, like the burnt raspas Abuela would never serve, like dark chocolate but more bitter. I brewed pure espresso in my own juices, straining brown water through my teeth, spitting the grounds when they had given up most of their flavor. The buzz was beatific. I didn't feel the five-kilometer walk. Darkness, so firm and affirming a master on a night of new moon, enfolded me—my world, the valley—in a magnificent wing. The underside was spotted with sentient stars, at the center: the ox and plow. An oil lamp flickered here or there at a hacienda, but it might have been a star instead. Darkness cloaked the mogotes, those immortal leviathans, for a billion nights over their lifetimes of prostrate rumination.

The wing abruptly lifted and blades of light flew under and in. I kept my head down and focused on the jagged line between grass and packed earth. A truck roared past spitting dust, and the driver shouted an insult. I didn't turn when they came up from behind. I didn't want anyone to stop and offer a ride. The wing settled again and the night nestled in. The quiet. The crickets. Houses with broad and inviting porches stared each other down across the narrow avenue.

I was invited in to sit in front of the box with the entire family—luckily she had no brothers to tease me—and none of them paid any attention to us since *it's starting! it's starting!* The novela that night was one of the worst: bad actors baldly trying to upstage each other with camp dialogue shouted across dislocated scenes. Plus, it was Argentine. All the actors lisped. I touched my date's hand and she jumped in her rocking chair, darting a vacant look at me. I'd torn her out of the world of la tele; she had forgotten I was there. I told her I had to go back to the bohío. She whispered to come see her the next night, to meet in the yuca patch after the house was dark. Nobody in the family noticed me slip out.

A moonless wandering up and down the avenue, agonizing over an alienation originating entirely within myself but aggravated by the novela, blaring accusations—"*Yo sé que me traicionas*"—and insinuations—*"Te quiero, Raul. Aunque me mate, te quiero"*—from all the houses in the town, from all across the island.

The next morning Manolito boasted over breakfast that, if he wanted, he could climb all the way up to the Tope de Viñales. When my uncle Antonio called him a liar, Manolito jumped up from the table without finishing his milk and roared, "Take a good look at me, brother, because I want you to remember what I looked like." He stormed out the door with my aunts clawing at his clothes. Abuela followed onto the patio and yelled after her youngest son, calling him caprichoso. Silently sipping his café, Abuelo ignored the outburst.

When he went rolling like thunder down into the valley, Manolito was wearing rubber boots, his green work pants, a faded red pullover, and a ragged palm hat.

Trying to keep spirits up for the rest of breakfast, Antonio bragged about his own prowess plumbing the caves, but everyone except for Abuelo was glum. Even Tío Antonio had sensed a haunting portent in his brother's final declaration. We children passed that day in gloomy anxiety, certain that we'd never see Manolito again. For the sisters, brothers, and the young cousins, Emilio and me, the mantle of sadness was heavier even than when Tía Sevilla had passed away. At least then we'd had the body to wail over, Sevilla's cold, captive beauty to console us. We went through our morning chores like a pack of walking zombies: sweeping the patio, feeding and tending to the animals, readying the places for lunch in dubious hope that Manolito might return. At midday there was an empty setting at the table. After lunch we all wrestled with siestas in the heat and fierce sun of the early afternoon. I dreamt of a lioness pouncing from the mouth of a cave and clamping her jaws around my leg. Her raw vise took hold and I heard Manolito's laughter reverberating from deep inside the mountain.

The sun accelerated in its precipitous descent toward the near peaks, which hulked over Abuelo's vega like a supine giant. I thought my own heart might extinguish with it. Abuela, in her supper preparations, was stoic. I couldn't tell whether she was in shock over the loss of her youngest or merely resigned to providing for the surviving eight. We all went in to eat, and suddenly, as if nothing about that day had been unusual, Manolito was there at his place in a clean shirt. Emilio and I fluttered around him, twittering, "¡Tío! ¡Tío!" Manolito was silent, stonefaced but for the perpetual wild look in his eye. He refused to rough-house with us or discharge his usual hyena whoops. What was wrong? Had something awful happened after all? Was this really our uncle? Antonio sat across from him and didn't dare open his mouth. We kids piped down. Manolito gobbled down his chícharo like a horse. Abuelo seemed to be suppressing a slender grin, a rare expression for him.

When the meal was almost over, Abuelo asked, "¿Y qué hiciste hoy, hijito?"

Shoveling the last of the beans from his bowl, Manolito replied, "The tope. I split the tip of that bitch in half." Antonio couldn't suppress a snort.

Abuelo got up from the table before café, something I'd never seen him do before, and went into his bedroom. He emerged with his sailor's spyglass, which he would take out only for special events like meteor showers and during the fiesta de San Juan to take in all the parties of the valley. Abuelo walked outside to the lip of the patio, and one by one we followed, leaving food on our plates. It was that half-hour of the day when the sun, so near to setting behind the giant's shoulders, irradiates the Tope de Viñales with all the brilliance of projected cinema.

Abuelo let Juan, the oldest, look first. "No veo nada," he said after a full minute.

"P'allá'riba, en la cima, a la altura del árbol."

Nearly a minute more and Juan said, "¡Coño!" Abuelo let us take turns, from oldest to youngest. We couldn't believe our eyes. At the heights of the Tope de Viñales, atop a tree that grew at the very summit, an unmistakable flag of pale red fabric: the shirt Manolito had been wearing when he left that morning. Back inside, Manolito threw back his coffee as he always did when he finished his meal at the end of a day of hard work.

That night I left the bohío wearing two pullovers. In the small garden behind my girlfriend's house, I took off both shirts, unraveling the one underneath and laying it out on the humid soil between rows of yuca. I put the outer shirt back on. She met me in the canopy of the yuca plant, which gives forth such extravagant foliage to thrust a humble plug of sustenance into even the stoniest earth. We greeted each other with our eyes. A smile: a smile. Great green fronds fluttered above us in the breeze, tickling her bare shoulders. I sat down among the stalks of rough, scaly bark and she stood over me. I saw the outline of her slim hips through the sheer fabric of the white nightgown. It was with a one-two flick that she stepped out of her underwear. She clutched them in a closed fist and fell forward, pushing my shoulders as she descended, knees clamped around my lower ribs, the undershirt a narrow blanket to keep her shins out of the dirt. She tugged my shorts to my knees.

Then she raised her gown. A delicate scallop of dark hair bearded the cleft between her legs. She parted the tuft with two fingers, sliding her vagina over my erection. Eyes rolled back beneath my closed eyelids, and she placed a cool finger to my lips. I moaned within. She did most of the work. It was quieter and more efficient. I was the sea and she was the ship. *Los hombres marineros*, I sang inside my head, lending a touch of absurdity to the erotic atmosphere so as not to explode before the lips of her mouth parted and she released the sweet breath of nectar she was learning to distill. She bent forward, covered me, and gave me an ambrosia kiss. Now she drank it back into herself. She saved it for the man she would marry, maybe.

She stood up, pulled on her underwear, and crouched beside me in the dirt. She planted a dry kiss on my cheek, right on my lunar, then turned and walked back to the house. Now I was allowed to finish myself, but I didn't. Where would I have put it? Imagination had made me hard. Imagination helped me lie there alone in the cold. I was lying on my back in a yuca patch in Viñales, and in my mind I had just done sex with Ojitos Lindos eight hundred kilometers away.

When I returned to school at the end of the summer, I found out Ojitos Lindos had left Havana. Her mother was from the other end of the island, so the widow had taken her child back to grow up among the soft-spoken, slow-moving guajiros of Oriente. Although my grandmother remained in the house, a teacher advanced me early to el pre-universitario, where I slept in a dormitory on the bunk above Yorki's. I often thought about Ojitos Lindos and wondered whether I'd ever look into those eyes again.

Eight years after our first encounter at the cemetery, I saw Ojitos Lindos when she returned to Havana to go to medical school. The eyes were unforgettable. By way of reintroduction, I identified myself in the library. "La Mancha, remember?" She smiled, her eyes flashing. I asked her to a movie. She surprised me by saying yes. I reminded her that my real name was Manolo, Mano for short. Her real name, I remembered, was Elena.

8 August 1992

In the morning we rose with the dawn and enjoyed steaming ajiaco drunk from plastic cones. "There's nothing better to strengthen you for the day," Manolito said. The broth is salty and bitter and contains every last part of the pig, some chunks bristly as a scrub brush. If you can gag it down, it helps take care of a hangover.

"¡Mono! Ven conmigo a ordeñar la vaca." Manolito untied the calf and towed him near enough to start his mother lactating. He tied the calf to a nearby tree and began cooing to the heifer. "VaaaaCA . . . vaaaaCA . . . VAca-VAca-vaaaaCA." Manolito jerked fulsome spurts from her swollen udders, filling a three-gallon bucket with steaming milk that frothed less than an inch from the top.

"Venga, Mono, you do it."

"No, Manolito. It's been too long."

Manolito insisted I get under there with him. I knew what was coming, but I indulged my uncle anyway. Manolito shot a hot jet of milk into my face. His hysterical laughter reverberated down the mountain, making cattle moo in the valley.

Before long Manolito set out on his mule. "It's time to take my muy muchacha to town." On Saturdays he gets himself a bottle of banana wine and goes off to Pinar, the entire thirty miles on la mula, not the horse, porque la mula knows her own way home.

After lunch Emilio changed into his coast guard uniform and we drove out to the marina. At the dock we boarded the lone cutter. We smoked a joint and motored out to where we could see the island taper to the narrowest lip of purple on the horizon, Cabo San Miguel. Gulf waters seal a political destiny when they turn right or left at the cape. Molecules either move north to the greenish Straits of Florida or south through the blue Yucatan Channel on their way to Haití and la República Dominicana: greener on the way to the land of the greenback, bluer to Curaçao. Emilio rolled another joint and I didn't feel at all seasick.

Ten miles out Emilio cut the engines. At sunset the sky and sea were blinding blue-bright, but the island was its own source of light. This was not just the sun shining off the leaves. This was the purple heart of the island itself. This was earth, sand, and mineral shining. With distended gaze drinking in the big picture, I thought I saw a gentle ripple in the terrestrial ridge. I couldn't be sure my eyes weren't playing tricks. "Son los mogotes de Viñales," Emilio said. "Either that or it's the rocks in your head."

Toward nightfall I nodded off to the gentle samba of the water, but just after dark something roared overhead and wrested me back to reality. An airplane had buzzed close above our boat, flying much lower than would be possible on land. The small dual-engine was less than a hundred feet from starboard when I was shocked to see something as big as a man drop from inside the black mouth on the side of the fuselage. Emilio gunned the engine, wheeling hand over hand to roll the rudder.

"¡Carajo! What was that?" I shouted over the engine. The airplane climbed, pulled west.

"What do you think?"

"Hermanos al Rescate?"

"No way, primo. That's the best Cesna there is. Los gusanos fly shitty little single-props."

Emilio pulled the cutter up alongside the float. I saw it was not a man, but a small burlap raft shrink-wrapped in plastic. My cousin hooked and hoisted it onto the deck, and I saw through the clear plastic: a man-sized bushel of marijuana. Emilio plunged his knife into the parcel and the vacuum seal popped to release a great gush of fragrance. Golden-haired buds coated over with crystals gave the flowerlets the look of shaggy confections, sugared like churros. I held a cured branch as thick and long as my arm. Emilio had to say only one word to enlighten me: "Colombians."

"Where do you get the money to pay for it?"

"I don't. They drop it free of charge. My socio on this detail is trustworthy, and he's got a friend who sells in Havana at a great profit."

We found a live crab in the folds of the burlap. "He's still crawling. He must have gotten in there wherever this bushel was wrapped."

"Maybe it was deliberate, Escobar's way of telling us it's fresh." Emilio threw the creature back into the sea. "Maybe he'll find himself a nice cangreja Cubana."

Back on land, Emilio filled two Tropicola bottles for my car from coast guard pumps. "I can help you out, you know, if you'd like to get some dolares."

"What would I need to do?"

"Drop something off with a friend in Havana. My socio and I need to find another reliable driver. Lately, there have been three or four deliveries a week."

"No, gracias."

"I wouldn't offer if I didn't think you'd be perfect with your state Lada and your medical card. Just once or twice. It's an easy two hundred dollars a run."

"If they caught me, they wouldn't just put me in jail. They'd take away my doctor's license."

"When you get out, you could make more as a taxista."

"That's the joke these days."

"It's no joke."

Near midnight we were back in the Lada on the narrow, winding road into the mountains. Something ahead was holding up traffic. Around the curve we saw Manolito's mule and our stinkpotted tio loco strapped in the saddle, draped like a blanket over the animal's neck, hands clasped behind her ears, snoring but somehow hanging on. A line of buses and taxis, their lights blazing and horns blaring, couldn't pass the struggling beast.

Lada and mule made it back to Abuelo's vega before dawn. Manolito was so drunk that Emilio and I, getting him out of the saddle, could only let him fall to earth. He lay on the ground snoring. Lydia served the cousins coffee in silence. She won't do anything to help Manolito when he gets like that, especially when he's been gone all night.

I lit a cigarette. "Find me a stick that's not too dirty," I told Emilio.

"What are you going to do?"

I didn't reply. I went to the well and came back with a bucket half-full of water. Emilio handed me the stick. Manolito breathed deeply and slowly, sleeping like a baby. Beneath his eyelids, his pupils bounced between the limits of lost worlds. He snorted once violently, making Emilio almost jump out of his skin, then settled back into a light snore.

"You're not going to throw water on his head, are you?" Emilio said. "If he wakes up wet he'll be very angry. Maybe he'll still be drunk and won't recognize you."

I stirred a cupful of sugar into the bucket. The women of the house, preparing breakfast, cast nervous glances from the bohío. I dipped the tip of the stick in the pail and raised the head of the dreaming drunk. A few drops of sugar water fell to his lips. Manolito's tongue came out in reflex to lick. He briefly reached with his lips and slumped back to earth. I dipped the stick again and Manolito's mouth closed around the end. He started to suck the wood. In five minutes, Manolito was awake and giving orders to everybody in the house, Emilio and me included. It was almost morning, and it was time to get to work.

9 August 1992

When I returned from Pinar on Sunday afternoon with a bag of Abuelo's chamomile tea, I found a note in the attic. Julia had gone out to pick up some things from her old apartment. I opened the French doors and realized my balcony had become a jungle. In a week Julia had brought my dead plants back to life. For the first time in a number of days I was alone in my attic, and I missed her: not Elena, not Carlota, but Julia. I busied myself with folding my clothes and setting out clean scrubs for my next shift at the pediátrico, but all the while I was waiting for her to get home.

Beatrice called up the stairs, "¡TeLÉfono!"

It was Julia. "Where are you calling from?"

"The turistienda down the street."

"Why don't you come up?"

"I don't want you to see me."

"Why not?"

"It's not pretty, Mano. I look ugly, very ugly."

I went down to meet her. She was crying and her face and hands were covered with scrapes and bruises.

"Alejandro followed me. He tore out fistfuls of my hair before I could run away. He smudged his burning cigarette out on my head . . ."

I took her to the clinic to clean her wounds with a saline solution and apply aloe to the lesions. I lay compresses on her bruised chest and shoulders and wrapped a bandage with a poultice around her head. Her earlobes and lips were red, and the red of her unpainted mouth ran a little around the edges to pink. She was running a high fever.

"We should call la patrulla," I told her.

"We can't. They take Alejandro's payoffs."

"I never should have left you alone."

I took her upstairs and put her to bed on the sofa. Curled up on the braided rug, I lay awake a long time listening to her shallow breath. Several hours and many cigarettes later, I fell asleep.

10 August 1992

Julia still had the bandage around her head when I got home from the pediátrico on Monday afternoon. She said it was comfort against the swelling, but I suspected that grief and shame had briefly brought her to a place where she had given up the wish to see. I asked, "Want me to read you something?"

"¿Algo de qué?"

"No sé. Un cuento o un poema."

"Con dos condiciones: as long as it doesn't have anything to do with medicine or la Revolución."

"No te preocupes." French doors shut, slats pulled against the sun, I took out the bright blue Bulfinch. She was skeptical at first, but lifting the lip of elastic fabric from over her eyes, she muttered that she would give any man a chance whose name meant camachuelo. I lit a cigarette and took Julia right into Prometheus and Pandora.

Woman was not yet made. The story is that Jupiter made her and sent her to Prometheus and his brother, to punish them for their presumption in stealing fire from heaven; and man, for accepting the gift. The first woman was named Pandora. She was made in heaven, every god contributing something to perfect her. Venus gave her beauty, Mercury persuasion, Apollo music, etc. Thus equipped, she was conveyed to earth, and presented to Epimetheus, who gladly accepted her, though cautioned by his brother to beware of Jupiter and his gifts. Epimetheus had in his house a jar, in which were kept certain noxious articles, for which, in fitting man for his new abode, he had had no occasion. Pandora was seized with an eager curiosity to know what this jar contained; and one day she slipped off the cover and looked in. Forthwith there escaped a multitude of plagues for hapless man—such as gout, rheumatism, and colic for his body, and envy, spite, and revenge for his mind—and scattered themselves far and wide.

By the second page Julia had propped herself up with pillows. "I like the sensibility of this Camachuelo fellow," she said. "The first woman was the midwife of all the world's plagues—the chief being horniness. Wouldn't you agree?"

"Certainly: a plague of epidemic proportions."

"Giving birth to man's dependency on the scarce and difficult-to-obtain antidote."

"Which is?"

"Pussy! Read on, doctor."

Julia and I were as hungry as the cats that live on the roof. I read to her from Bulfinch and we brewed Abuelo's tea leaves over and over. Julia lay back on the sofa and folded my clothes. She fished in the pockets of a pair of dirty pants and found the dollar change Director González had given me at his coctail party. Julia took a pen and inked something on the face of the bill.

"What's that?"

She laughed.

"What are you drawing on that dollar?"

She finished what she was doing to the bill and balled it up for better throwing. It bounced off my nose. I uncrumpled the bill and saw what she had found so funny. Jorge Washington had a Havana-shaped mark on his right cheek; block letters to the left of his froglike smirk read: *Soy homosexual.*

Julia laughed. She fell asleep on the sofa and I curled up on the rug.

11 August 1992

On Tuesday I left the pediátrico and picked up a couple of cucumbers at the mercado libre. I rinsed them in the kitchen and asked Julia, "Do you know where the scalpel is?"

"I was using it to cut some pictures out of a magazine." She rose from the cushions. Before I realized what was happening, she stepped up behind me, pressed her lips to the back of my neck, and whispered, "Oye, hijo de puta, don't you want to fuck me?" I finally gave in.

We were dreaming awake, and it was only a moment until I was stiff as a rail and putting on a condom and pulling her up by her shoulders, lifting her up on top of me, no time to take underwear off—she tugged the fabric aside and looked me in the eyes. Her face concealed none of her avaricious ambition. There was no fight in me, and she didn't have to prey with such ferocity, yet I was touched by that look, a reminder that I was desirable, not just a creature of habit going through autoerotic motions with expert manipulations. She was generous and omnivorous. My eyes rolled back in my head. Her eyelids fluttered and I caught a glimpse of her expression, spontaneously contented. It was the slightest contraction of her cervix that reawakened my heart to what zealous youth can do.

I tried to keep from coming. I thought of baseball, of the European Common Market, of histology. I thought of Fidel; I thought of a hall full of agronomists falling asleep during El Comandante's speech on cucumber production, and nevertheless I succumbed. When I finished she kept going. Beneath her I felt like a dead thing, like I had gotten the life sucked out of me. There was something terrible about the way she kept moving.

When it was done, I could see she was weary and remote, and a tide of guilt washed over me. "I wasn't after sex. I just wanted to help you."

"Don't be so stuck," she said, with a swat to my lunar. "You should have several girlfriends."

Julia and I settled into the pile of cushions and blankets on the floor and stayed up all night. Each time she rose to go to the bathroom, the arc of her naked butt swung overhead like a churchbell. Each time I lit a cigarette, I lit one for her too. We made up a game called *Imagináriamericanos*.

"If we were Americans, I'd have my own apartment," she said. "Your turn."

"If we were Americans, I'd practice medicine in a clean hospital."

"I'd just show up with the money, and the landlord would let me move right in."

"A sparkling, sanitized hospital, walls and floors that haven't even heard of bacteria."

"If we were Americans, I'd invite you over for coffee, and you'd bring flowers."

"If we were Americans, I'd drive to and from the hospital, and the gas tank would always be full."

"There wouldn't be any monotony. There would always be a choice."

"If we were Americans, I'd save my money and buy a coffee plantation."

We lay on the cushions silently for several minutes with heads touching, El Ché's beard and mouth, upside-down, looking like a black mountain looming above a dark lake. What they don't tell you about when you cheat on someone, even someone you don't like very much: For a long time afterwards the guilt can be like a dead body you carry alongside you. And when she finally leaves, the body becomes her, her memory.

Julia said, "You feel a ghost, I know."

"How can you tell?"

"You think I haven't felt her too?"

I lit a cigarette and lay awake a long time, awkward in my underwear, listening to her breath and watching my fingers twitch at my side.

O

---

12 August 1992

Wednesday after my shift I told Julia, "Come with me to the necropolis."

"Why?"

"I want to show you something."

"I hate that place. I hate all cemeteries."

I said, "Today's my birthday."

Julia frowned. "All right, I'll go."

En Cemeterio Colón, workers with mops and buckets cleaned the stones on the main road. I took Julia to my mother's tomb at the corner of H y 8. The sounds of cars and trucks so far away, we stood for a minute without speaking. Nearby, an old woman swept leaves off her husband's slab.

I told Julia, "It was on my birthday that I got this lunar on my face."

"I thought it was a birthmark."

"That's the little lie I tell grown-ups, but birthmarks occur at birth. My mark was born of a small hemorrhage I survived as a child."

"What's the lie you tell children?"

"That a bird dropped it on me."

"Follow me," Julia said. "There's something I want to show you." She took me to a corner of the necropolis where I'd never been. J y 14, a communal crypt inscribed: *Asociación de Reporteros de la Habana*. At the back of the antechamber was a wall of glass, still intact, two inches thick. A door of the same glass, hanging on rust-blackened hinges, led to a dark stairway. It took all my strength to pry the door open. We followed the glow of my father's lighter down the stone stairs. At the bottom, Julia pushed open a wrought-iron gate. The subterranean chamber was cold and lightless. Cracks in the walls let a noxious miasma seep in. Strong odors of clay and decay made me breathe through my mouth.

The floor was strewn with femurs, ribs, pelvises—everything but skulls, which fetch a decent price among practitioners of Palo Monte. Shreds of decomposing clothing matted to brown bones. Graffiti: *ME CAGO EN DIOS. WELCOM TU DE MACHIN.* In a hole in the stone floor lay a headless skeleton. At the center of the room three feet off the floor was a slab three feet wide, seven feet long. This is where they would rest the coffin while readying the appropriate tomb, a waystation making it easier on the pallbearers' backs and less upsetting to the family if there was any kind of delay. There is something terrible about laying a coffin on the floor. Footstones, stacked five wide by four tall, covered most of the west wall. The north and east walls would probably have fit forty more corpses, but the cement had never been broken, probably because Fidel came along and the Asociación de Reporteros de la Habana was disbanded shortly thereafter. The dead that would have filled this monument went into exile.

"When I joined Alejandro's crew they brought me here," Julia said.

"What for?"

"Initiation. First they get you high on stolen painkillers, gasoline vapors, even livestock tranquilizers." She told me a story.

They blindfold you and lead you down a long stairway. All you can sense is the unwholesome thickness to the air, a sulfuric moisture that makes you gag. From the corners, the stale stink of many years of urine. And the damp cold. They make you sit on the slab. Here is your fiancé. He's wearing a glove. Hold his hand. You smell the wax of candle flames. Do you take this man to be your husband? Say I do or they will hit you. They won't let you in. They will kill the little dog you like so much. I do. Come lie down beside him. You feel his hard shoul-

der against yours. He still hasn't said anything. Turn
and kiss him. His leathery lips don't kiss back. The
stifled laughter of the others in your crew echoes
hollowly off the walls. I now pronounce you husband
and wife. The blindfold is snapped off your face and
the other girls, your new sisters, all laugh. They hold
candles, and by their light you see your betrothed. A
moan of revulsion catches in your throat, taps bile.
You vomit once violently, gasp, vomit again. This air
is not for breathing. Now you know why it is foul.
Your new family's cruel laughter echoes off the stone
walls, and your priest, the pimp, cries, "Casados hasta
que la muerte los separe." Again you vomit. Someone
pushes your face to his and your arms flail. Your husband's skull rolls off the slab away from the mummified cadaver and across a floor strewn with condoms,
bottles, syringes, feces, and bones. When it's time to
leave, the chulo takes the skull away with him. It
never belonged to the mummy in the first place.

"This place is horrible, Julia. Let's get out of
here."

By the time we were back at the attic, Julia was
crying in my face: "¿Porqué quieres que esté aquí?"

"What do you mean?"

"I don't have to stay, you know. I can go. Please
tell me, Mano: Why are you letting me stay here?"

"I don't know why," I told her, "but I don't want
you to go away."

"You've got your hand inside me, clutched around my heart. Now you're ripping it out. You monster!"

Julia picked up a porcelain ashtray and threw it at my head. It bounced off the wall and broke in pieces on the floor. I was still recovering from the surprise when she rushed toward me. I thought: She's just a child; she must be coming to apologize. But before I realized what was happening Julia picked up a jagged chunk of the ashtray from the floor and slashed at my face, crying, "¡Hijo de puta!" My hand shot up in reflex and I received a gash down the length of my forearm. I grabbed her arms and she shrieked, her face disfigured in a mask of bitter hatred. Kicking and spitting she tried to break free. Air caught in her larynx, contorting her scream into a grotesque, primal howl and transforming the sound into a sob as she collapsed to the floor in tears, bringing me to my knees beside her, my hands still clutching her wrists. I held her in a close embrace. She was sobbing, saying, "I'm sorry, Mano . . . Tu cumpleaños . . ." With whispered entreaties for measured breaths, I coaxed Julia back from the edge of hyperventilation. I cleaned and dressed the wound on my arm, and Julia fell asleep in my embrace.

O

---

13 August 1992

When I got back from the pediátrico on Thursday, Julia was gone. "Where did she go?" I asked aloud, but El Ché had stopped speaking to me. I waited up all night, but she didn't come. The next day before work I walked to the cinderblock complex named after Máximo Gómez and asked the block captain about Tonia and her family. "The girl with the abscess?" She pointed me to their apartment.

"Hola, señora. Do you remember me?"

"Como no, doctor: You saved my daughter's life. My husband and I have wanted to come to the hospital to thank you. We owe you our lives, and I'm sorry I haven't come see you yet. Life gets so busy."

"Please don't worry about it. How is your daughter doing?"

"All well, gracias a Dios. Please come in. There's no coffee, but I can offer you chamomile tea."

"I appreciate the offer, but in fact I have very little time. I want to ask whether you can help me find someone."

"I hope I can help."

"That night at the hospital, after the surgery, your niece came in to thank me."

"My niece?"

"Yes. She brought me a sandwich and told me your daughter was her favorite cousin."

"That's strange, because my husband and I have no niece."

"I see."

"Perhaps we should report this to the vigilance committee."

"I wouldn't bother. It was probably just a friend from school who loves your daughter like a cousin."

"Maybe. What was her name?"

"Julia, about sixteen years old."

"Doesn't sound familiar, but I can ask Tonia when she wakes up."

"Don't bother. It was probably just a mix-up."

"I'm sorry I couldn't be of help, doctor."

I waited up all night, but Julia didn't come.

After my Friday shift at the pediátrico, I walked to Yorki's apartment. My knock woke him from a nap. "¡Coño, Mano! I was dreaming about food." He pulled his pants on and donned his sunglasses.

"You're not going to believe this. Last night a guy I haven't seen before comes around and whispers to me, 'Oye, compañero, aquí tengo unas exquisitas chuletas empanizadas.' Of course I don't believe him, but he shows one to me and my mouth starts watering. There it is, still frozen—a breaded steak! He says they were stolen from the kitchen at the Cohíba. So I buy two: ¡Coño! Ten fucking dollars! When I get them into the kitchen and start frying them up with an old onion rind, something doesn't smell right."

"No me digas . . ."

"¡Empanadas de toalla! ¡Carajo! A hard day's hustles wasted on a couple of breaded dishtowels!"

"These thieves have gone too far. And the vigilantes of the CDR are no better, spreading rumors about ground glass in the black-market bread. Kids are starving while they mess with our heads."

"¡Bajo! ¡Bajito!" Yorki whispered, then asked, "What's eating you, Mano?"

"The jinetera I helped out—she took off yesterday."

"She's probably in some kind of trouble, and then it's probably best that she split. I wouldn't give her another thought if I were you, Mano. The important thing is that you got laid. You did fuck her, didn't you?" I said nothing. "Don't tell me you didn't get it while you had the chance . . . Just remember, it's you who did the fucking and she who got fucked."

"Oye, Yorki, can I borrow your moped for a few hours?"

"I need it tonight, but you can use it tomorrow as long as you put some gas in it."

"I'll siphon a liter out of the Lada."

"I'll leave it parked in the alley. Remember to pretend to use a key in case any of the neighborhood kids are watching. I don't want them to catch on and steal it."

When I got back to the attic I found that Julia still hadn't returned, so I went down to the clinic to lie on a cot. A brief thundershower came and went, and then I heard a crack of glass. I peered around the curtain and saw the broken window pane, the overcoat sleeve, and the glove belonging to Detective Perez, chief homicide investigator of the PNR, he of the exquisite manicure.

15 August 1992

On Saturday afternoon when I close up the policlínico, there's no sign of Julia and the black Toyota with tinted windows is still parked on Calle 23. The strangest thing about the unexpected interview with Perez is that it did not end in my arrest. The number-two man at the PNR has nothing to lose by locking up a Cuban doctor for a few days. And murder is not a common crime in this country. Although sudden bursts of violence, manslaughter by hit and run, and even accidental poisoning with homemade liquor occur with some frequency, the premeditated, plotted art of murder has been effectively suppressed by a government that doesn't permit private ownership of firearms. The PNR investigates with zero tolerance to the most isolated act of homicide. There is no cold case. Unsolved murder in the first degree remains an aberration of the Yanquis to the north.

Under the scrutiny of a nationwide neighborhood vigilance network, a militarized police force, and an army of forensics specialists trained by Cold War–era KGB experts, Cuba is an island of already-captive suspects. No matter how quickly a perpetrator might flee, there's only so far to run and nowhere to hide. Anyone who would attempt exile is faced with a perilous passage over turbulent seas. Many criminals have served themselves justice—and saved Fidel the expense of their incarceration—by taking to makeshift rafts in treacherous swells. The sharks of the Florida Straits are famously well fed.

I siphon a Tropicola bottle full of gas from the Lada and leave the house through the alley. The ignition on Yorki's moped broke shortly after he bought it, but he bypassed a few wires and now it starts with just a kick. I pantomime the key routine and give it a running start down the street.

I ride all over the city, crisscrossing the necropolis, cutting across Centro Habana and circling Coppelia, riding behind the Habana Libre and puttering up the hill between the fallout catacombs and the empty playing fields of the university. I descend La Rampa with glances down all the side streets. I turn right on Malecón, past the Oficina de Intereses, the Hotel Nacional, the pedestal where in '59 the mobs tore down the American eagle and Picasso's promised dove never nested. Night is falling when I near the end of the sea wall and turn up Paseo del Prado, climbing the hill past the bronze lions, the iron lampposts, the stone benches across from the Ministry of the Interior where people barter apartment swaps. My heart is beating hard when el Capitolio comes into view. The street across from the Capitol steps is empty but for a few parked turistaxis. At the Parque Central, I park the bike and sit for a minute on a bench. There are many lovely girls looking for a date, but Julia is not among them.

From the crest of the hill I can see Morro Castle half-cloaked in silver and black clouds that promise rain but not before morning. I ride down Carlos III and take a shortcut through Quinta de los Molinos to avoid the military detachment at the Palacio de la Revolución. There are no lights on anywhere in the thicket behind La Madriguera, and the dwarf palms comb my hair as I ride through the urban jungle of the park. I take Paseo over the hill back for another pass on Malecón, following the sea wall west this time. I ride through the tunnel to Miramar and search among the girls along Quinta Avenida. Turistaxis speed past me on their way to Marina Hemingway. Some slow to shine headlights on small groups of jineteras, girls in shorts and Spandex who blaze briefly in the high beams and are extinguished like candle flames. I ride all the way out to the marina and then turn onto

Primera, where I let the sea spray blow me back to Vedado.

I park the moped in the alley behind Yorki's apartment and go upstairs to let him know I've left a little gas in the tank. He claps his hands together and says, "Did you hear the one about Pepito? One day at school, the teacher asks all the students what they eat at home. Pepito says, 'I eat rice and beans but my mother likes eating palitos.' 'Sticks? Are you sure, Pepito?' 'Sí, maestra . . . Every night I hear her in the bedroom telling my father, '¡Ai, qué palo tan rico!'" Yorki takes off his shades for a second to rub his eyes. "Mano, I've got to tell you something: Me caso."

"Now *that's* a good one!"

"I'm not kidding. I'm getting married."

"What? Just like that?"

"I've been thinking about it for a while."

"What are you talking about? You used to tell me that you'd never let yourself get nailed."

Yorki grins. "That was last week."

"At least tell me it's un casamiento jinetero: an Americana or something who'll take you across with her."

"Why should it concern you? Just because we went fishing for pango doesn't mean I'm a maricón."

"Quit talking so much shit. You think a wife is going to let you go out at night, even if it's not to search for girlfriends?"

"Don't think that I won't, although she might think she's not letting me."

"Precisely my point. I know you too well, Yorki. We go out walking. We have a good time. But the moment you're married you're going to turn crazy trying to cheat on your wife. You'll spend all your free time womanizing."

"There's more to life than sex, Mano. A man needs to make a good couple. I want someone to take care of my house and clean my clothes. I want sons. And what's more, this woman and I fuck really well. It's gotten to the point where I'm afraid she might make me faithful."

"Well, what can I say, Yorki? I wish you a happy marriage. Really."

Yorki averts his sunglasses to face the Florida Straits. "Mano, it's Carlota."

I put my hand on the arm of his sofa and sit. All I can think to say is *hijo de puta*, but I don't let the phrase escape my mouth because I know it's meant for me.

16 August 1992

By Sunday afternoon there's still no sign of Julia, so I walk the alleys to Paseo and climb the hill to the terminal. "¿Último?" The last in line lifts a hand. I make la cola and catch the last bus to the beach.

I am pressed against an old woman, between us a live chicken she has hypnotized by the way she holds its feet. "Y tu: ¿adónde vas?"

"Para Guanabo."

"It's too late to take a swim. By the time we get there, the sun will be going down and you'll have to turn back."

I walk around the beach at sunset watching turistas pair up with jineteras and jineteros. After dark I hang around one of the hotels until the girls and boys begin emerging from the rooms. Some of the kids congregate at the cabanas, curling up together to keep warm against the breeze. Nobody has seen

Julia, but one girl remembers her. "Julia la rubia? She hasn't worked this beach for more than a year. The bitch owes me money."

I pass a sleepless night curled up beneath a palapa and take the first bus of the day back to Havana. I walk straight to the pediátrico and the black Toyota is there, parked outside admitting.

It is a full day of consultations. The nurse preps each patient with vitals and a brief interview. Near the end of my shift she says, "Next one complains of eczema on her chest, but when I asked to see she says she will only show the doctor. She's probably a little old for the pediátrico. Should I send her to Hermanos Almejeiras?"

"No. I'll see what I can do for her. You can go ahead and get ready for the shift change."

I shut the curtain behind me, but I can hear the next patient sniffling just a few feet away. Privacy is impossible, even at a whisper. "Lift the front of your shirt, please." I take out my diagnostic pad and write: *Police out front, Toyota.*

Julia shakes her head. She has dyed her hair jet-black. She takes the pad and pen: *I came in back, ambulance dock.*

I write: *Did you do it?*

Julia scribbles furiously: *No! How could I?*

I write: *3 Monos, 10 minutos.* Julia nods. "You can put your shirt back on. Apply this cream twice a day after cleaning with mild soap and rinsing with clean water. Come back if it doesn't clear up."

Julia goes out through the back. I ask the incoming nurse to cover for me and leave the hospital by the ambulance station.

We meet at a nearby hotel that caters to tourists and jineteras. In the lobby she stands to meet me, and we are walking purposefully across the marble floor toward each other when a third person interposes himself. It's the head waiter, having crept out of the hotel restaurant for his requisite intervention, a gambit at protracting the presumed foreigner's fleecing: "¿Quisieran comer?" The entrance opens onto a bright, empty dining room full of gleaming china, sparkling crystal, and glowing linen napkins.

I cast an eye to the opposite wall and spy a sign beside a dark door. "¿Por qué no pasamos al bar?" I say to Julia without acknowledging the meddlesome waiter. "Seguro," says the camarero, his arm around her shoulder, already ushering her to the door to Los Tres Monos. Entering the cave from the full flare of the glass-walled lobby makes it feel even darker than it is. Holding my hand, Julia leads me to the corner booth. She waves the bartender off and runs her hand through my hair, her fingers trembling.

"While you were at the pediátrico on Thursday," she whispers in my ear, "one of the girls saw me on your balcony and called up that Alejandro was dead."

I want to light a cigarette but my hands are shaking. I press my lips to her ear. "Why didn't you go to the police?"

Julia whispers, "Tito and Jochi, the black brothers, are trying to blame it on me."

"I went to the house of the girl I operated on the night we met, the one you told me was your cousin."

"I'm sorry I didn't tell you the truth from the start, Mano, but I needed a reason to ask you about the HIV test. I come from out in the provinces. I don't have anyone in Havana. Nobody but you."

"I'll talk to the PNR. The homicide chief, Perez, might be able to help."

"Perez—that's the one Alejandro worked for! Ese tipo es muy malo! He takes bribes from all the chulos."

"Carajo, this country is going to shit. He broke into my clinic the other day."

"Don't you see, Mano? They're setting me up for this. I make a perfect scapegoat because I was trying to get out of prostitution. I need help. I need to leave Cuba. I'll take a raft if I have to."

"That would be suicide. The straits are too dangerous. You would need to get on a real boat with an experienced pilot."

"That costs hundreds—American hundreds."

"I might know someone who can help out. Where are you hiding?"

"I can't tell you. I don't want you to have trouble later. But I better not go out again in daylight." She tilts a look toward the bartender, who is polishing wine glasses. "And we can't meet here. Go to the place we visited your mother on your birthday. Come before dawn, between 4 and 5 in the morning. If there's any trouble I'll fold a message in the cracks of the cement. Do you have any cigarettes?"

"Take these." I hand her a half-pack of Populares. Julia gives me a quick kiss on the mouth, stands up, and walks briskly out of the bar.

I head back to the hospital to call Pinar del Rio, my heart pounding and the phone trembling in my hand. Emilio answers and I say, "Hola, primo, you remember that fresh crab we talked about?"

"Sure, Mano. How about tonight? I'll see you at the dinosaur—the hour Abuelo was born minus one."

"Good. Paco's going to need a drink."

"I'll bring some Tropicola. Hasta luego."

I leave the hospital through admitting and walk back to the house in Vedado, not bothering to look over my shoulder to spot the black Toyota. Up in the attic I shut the curtains on the French doors and grab a blanket. I go down the service stairs to the alley and pop the trunk of the Lada. Then I wrap Hernán in the blanket and carry him back up the service stairs. In the attic I put a sweatshirt on him, pull the hood over his skull, and place him in the rocking chair. Crouching to the floor, I inch the chair closer to the French doors until Hernán's shadow is silhouetted against the closed curtains. I hold a rung and gently rock the chair, keeping this up for five minutes. Then I take a fresh pack of Populares and some matches from the kitchen and head back down to the Lada. When I drive across Calle 12 at 25th, I can see the black Toyota parked across from my house two blocks away, cigarette smoke curling from the cracked passenger window.

On the outskirts of Marianao I barter my father's lighter for four liters of gas. Crosses stand vigil wherever cars skidded fatally off the pavement and into the ditches on the highway to Pinar del Rio. Cool air blows through the window gaps, but my hands keep sweating for the entire ride.

At 11 o'clock there is nobody on the streets of Pinar. The teenage metalheads are all crowded into the courtyard of the Joven Club, and everyone else has gone home to fall asleep in front of the novelas. When I walk behind the Natural History Museum to the small park in back, Emilio's voice comes out of nowhere. "Aquí en el techo."

I step around the brontosaurus and climb the ladder to the museum roof.

Emilio pulls a paper package and a plastic sack

out of an air duct. We crouch out of sight of the street. "It's vacuum-wrapped beneath the paper, so there's virtually no odor. When you get to Miramar, park near the mouth of the Almendares tunnel and walk straight to the northern loop of Quinta Avenida. Don't try to drive up to the drop, or you'll have a hard time getting around the cement barriers. You'll see a silver pickup truck with tinted windows and two inflated inner tubes in back, the kind fishermen float in. One tube will have a decoy package that looks just like this one resting in the center. Move purposefully as if you are about to walk past the pickup, then stop abruptly to tie your shoelace, wedging this package snugly in the center of the empty inner tube. When you rise be sure to pick up the decoy package. It will be much lighter than this one. Keep walking. Walk all the way to the beach without looking back. Don't talk to anyone. Don't look at anybody. Throw the empty package into the sea. Here, this is for Paco." Emilio gives me the plastic sack: four two-liter cola bottles filled with gasoline. "And this is for you." He hands me the money, a fat roll of American twenties I put down the front of my pants.

"Oye, primo, what's the possibility you could help me and a friend leave?"

"Leave? Leave where?"

"Leave the island. Leave Cuba," I tell him.

"What are you talking about? You've never even left that depressing attic in Vedado. Now you want to go to el otro lado?"

"A doctor can always find work."

"Not without an American license. Do you know what your father does up there? Old gusanos pay him fifteen dollars for a half-hour visit. He has to listen to their egotistic bullshit and dole out prescriptions to a black-market pharmacy run by some Marielito."

"It's complicated, Emilio. There's a girl who got set up."

"Coño, Mano, whenever you take on a woman it's like you're marching to your doom."

"Is it possible or not?"

"Where is she now?"

"In Havana."

"We'd never make it out of there. It's a whole different fleet, not friendlies."

"What if I brought her here, to the coast?"

"Carajo, hombre, call me tomorrow and I'll see what I can do. Just don't fuck this one up, all right?" He puts the paper package in my hands. "You won't have any trouble in Havana. They know you're my cousin. But don't get stopped on the drive. Stay under the speed limit."

I climb down from the roof of the museum, put the package in the trunk, and empty the cola bottles full of gasoline into my tank. It's almost midnight by the time I get back on the Carretera Central to Havana.

The Lada is running on fumes when I park it near the end of Quinta Avenida and begin walking up the middle of the boulevard with my package. There, near the mouth of the tunnel, is the pickup truck, inner tubes and the decoy package in back. I put the package Emilio gave me in the center of the empty tube, heart pounding and hands trembling while I pretend to tie my shoe. Then I stand up and walk away with the other package—it is lighter, probably empty. Home free! But when I am half a block away on C Street, someone behind me calls, "¡Señor!" A man's voice. I walk faster without turning to look. "¡Oye, señor!" The slapping of shoes on pavement: He is running after me. Anticipating that awful sound, someone calling a militant command: *¡Carné!* A random questioning and personal search. Don't look back. Walk straight to the sea.

He catches up with me, grabbing my elbow. "Amigo . . . ¿No buscas una chica?"

"¡Pendejo!" I tear my arm away from the chulo, a skinny mulatto, and fumble with the decoy package. "¡Quítate!"

"¡Coño! Sorry, compañero. I thought you were a tourist."

I move briskly to the sea, drop the decoy package, and turn back toward Quinta Avenida. From the walkway above the tunnel mouth, I see that the silver pickup is gone. I am tired, thirsty, and as hungry as always, but I have to make it across Vedado before dawn, so I walk through the tunnel and along the east bank of the pestilent river. I climb the chain-link fence, cross the small boatyard, and climb out the other side a few blocks from Calle Zapata, crossing far down the hill from the front gates of the necropolis. When I reach the low part in the concrete wall, I choose a shadowy place and boost myself over the wrought-iron fence of Cemeterio Colón.

I walk to the corner of H y 8. "Julia?" No answer. I run my fingers over the cement and feel a wadded slip of paper wedged tightly in a crack. I unfold it and hold it up to the light of a full moon. Julia's handwriting: *Medianoche, puerto*. The meeting place is at the Port of Havana. Midnight means we'll lose an entire day. I hope she's okay. No way I can go home now. I'll have to lay low all night, get to a cabina before sunrise, and call in sick at the pediátrico. I slip the note in my pocket with the money and lie down beside my mother's tomb to rest.

12 August 1979

T'en candles on a cake, right in front of my face. Chocolate: my favorite. The cake was small but special. It was not from the panadería or the lady down the street, who made the same cake for all the boys and girls. Mamá had made this one herself. She was strangely cheerful, singing, and Machado was dancing on his back legs. Spinning the cake, Mamá lit each candle with a straw she held in a trembling hand. While the cake went around I counted to ten, but I couldn't remember if I had counted the first candle already. Singing "Las Mañanitas," Mamá kept turning the plate, and I counted the candles on their second rotation: *eleven, twelve, thirteen, fourteen, fifteen* . . . If I kept counting, could I continue time traveling? Could I keep flying through the years from birthday to birthday? I blew out the flames, making a wish for Mamá to get better for good.

My mother cut the cake right in half and we ate off the same plate. We didn't even use forks. "It's your birthday, so we get to eat with our hands." Under the chocolate there was a sour flavor that made my tongue curl up. "Isn't it good?" she asked. It wasn't very good. I didn't want to hurt her feelings, so I said yes and put a little more in my mouth. While Mamá shoveled the crumbs from the plate, I spit out most of my piece and let Machado quietly gulp the half-chewed offering.

Two hours later, my mother and I were lying side-by-side on stretchers. Terrible pain shot through my abdomen. Mamá was unconscious, and the doctor was trying to get me to speak. "¿Qué fue, niño? ¿Qué tomaron? ¿O fue algo que te dieron de comer?"

"Un pastelito." Saying the words plunged knives into my gut.

"¿De qué era el pastelito?"

"Chocolate."

"¿Quién lo preparó?"

"Mi Mamá."

The doctor turned back on my mother and began pounding her chest. A nurse said, "The police told me that their dog was poisoned too."

The doctor told the nurse to get an orderly to open Machado up and find out what was in the cake. He took a long tube like a yellow water snake and forced it into the back of my throat. I gagged and my esophagus began convulsing, emptying my stomach of Aurora's peanuts. My mother never woke up. She had crushed a full bottle of her chemotherapy pills and mixed them into the cake. My own mild overdose caused a severe hemorrhage beneath the right eye: *Havana Lunar*.

18 August 1992

"Doctor." A voice, a man's, awakens me with a start. Eyes open on Tito, the younger of the two black brothers who worked for Alejandro. "Where is she hiding, feo?"

"No sé."

"Liar."

I dart a look around. We are in a narrow pocket between three tombs. Tito has me penned in.

"This is going to go a lot easier for you if you tell me where she is."

"I don't know."

Tito shows me what he's going to hit me with: an unvarnished nightstick. He steps forward and says, "Sueña con los angelitos, doctor."

I cover my head and roll, but he catches the base of my skull. A rocket bursts and goes dark, then there goes the darkness: one blackout wrapped in another.

* * *

Awaken to blackness, pain pulsing from temple, pinned beneath a leathery sack. Paralyzed. Air humid, thick with noxious gas. Stench. Shallow breath. Salivating. No light. Blink. No light at all for eyes.

"¿Hola?" Echo high and hollow. Cold stone. Alone. Push. Sack shifts. One arm, another. Roll ragged thing to stone. Bones. Keep calm. Rise. Feel around, find a wall.

A blind, squatting back-and-forth across the stone floor, kicking and batting after something. A wrought-iron gate secured with a clunky Russian padlock. Find something metal to strike against it. Only dry leaves, brittle bones—quadriceps, femur, thigh bone—and mummified remains. I don't need the dim light that seeps down to the chamber during the day to know: the smell tells me, and so does the slab in the center of the chamber. This is the crypt where Alejandro initiated his jineteras.

"Julia?" Echo and no more. Touch top of head: a substantial swelling, pain. Lie down again. Search pocket. Money and Julia's note still there. Tito never checked.

The stairs take on a violet glow in daytime, reflecting light from the glass-walled antechamber to the top of the landing. I needed water before I came here, but now my mouth is dry like cotton. I rattle the bars, stop to listen, cry, "¡Socorro!" I hear bus brakes and airplanes above, sometimes a distant shout echoing off the stones, but my cries provoke no response. Planning to meet here was stupid. *Medianoche, puerto.* I have to get out before midnight. Have to get someone's attention. Dry leaves scattered on the floor. I'd give all the money in my pocket to have my father's lighter back.

Try to sleep but the slab is very cold. Want a blanket but there are only bones. Spend the dark day at the edge of hallucination. Line up thoughts. Piece it back together. Find a way out. Out of this hell.

* * *

I am shocked awake by the flick of a lighter, the sudden appearance of Tito at the bottom of the stone stairway. I sit up with a start and shield my eyes from the bright flame. "You don't have to tire yourself out with shouting. There's a glass wall at the top of the stairs. Nobody will even hear a scream." Tito lets the lighter go out and stands smoking a cigarette on the other side of the gate. "Where is she hiding?"

"I don't know."

"¿Quizás en Miramar? Near Quinta Avenida? A friend of mine was working the neighborhood around the tunnel last night, and when he recognized that hideous mark on your face he followed you here." Tito takes a long drag of the cigarette. "But first he saw you throwing something in the ocean. What was in the box, doctor? Alejandro's head?"

"I didn't have anything to do with it and neither did Julia."

"Is that the name she gave you?"

"I need water."

"No water."

Throat is dry. Dry leaves. Thinking: *Medianoche, puerto*. "Can I have a cigarette?"

Tito lights one for me and passes it through the bars: mentholated Popular. "I'm going to watch you put it out when you're done. In fact, you're going to hand me the butt. If I have to come in there to get it, I'll crack your skull in half."

When it's down to the butt smoldering between pinched fingertips, I pass it back through the bars. Tito spits into the palm of his hand and puts it out. "Good doctor."

"I can give you money—dollars."

"You're a doctor; you don't have any money. Hasta mañana, feo." He climbs the dark stairs and calls from the top, "Or maybe pasado mañana."

* * *

When I lie very still on the slab in the center of the room, the flies begin landing on me, crawling over my face. I part my lips gently and a fly tests the crust at the corners of my mouth. I clamp my mouth shut and the flies scatter.

The light ebbs. The landing is lost in darkness. My clothes are damp with sweat and I feel cold. I anticipate each new stage of dehydration: a hangover headache, familiar enough, but aggravated by the lingering concussion. Sensitivity to hypothermia, orthostatic hypotension, severe dizziness each time I rise from the slab. Nothing to eat or drink and the migraine arrives. Think pleasant thoughts.

Eyes. An attempt at conjuring eyes. Only three or four women have really looked me in the eye. I'd like to be able to say *not counting Mamá*, but it wouldn't be true. Submerged deep in her room, her drugs, she never looked into anyone's eyes. Pero Aurora, sí. Even after the suicide. But her love was different. And then came Ojitos Lindos. I am sure she had experienced the connection before, but for me it was the first time. People rarely ever dared to look.

Agonizing hours pass. Midnight goes unmarked. Julia will think I stood her up. If I can get out of here she might come again tomorrow. I hold my last urine and struggle to resist the diarrhea. Keep alive. Keep alive long enough for someone to find me. Cold, clammy, no blanket, no jacket. The only way to sleep on this slab is like a corpse.

* * *

The stairs glow violet again and I begin to really thirst. Twenty-four hours. People should be wondering. Carlota? Not anymore. And Yorki will think I'm angry about her. Beatrice? Carajo . . . But I'm missing the second shift in two days at the pediátrico. The staff nurse will tell Director González that I didn't report. The director will tell the staff nurse to hold someone over. Then what? Back to his desk, his Marlboros and Belgian chocolate? Will he ask himself why Rodriguez, who hasn't missed a shift in more than a year, failed to call in?

The stone wall sweats with condensation. I try licking it. It is an unwholesome liquid, thick and alkaline, impregnated with the foul flavor of humus, but when my swollen tongue touches it the wetness is cool, comforting. The spongy papillae will absorb what water they can. Between licks I scrape the filth from my lips.

I walk around in circles to forestall atrophy. The pain in my bowels bends me double. I can't hold it any longer and go in the corner near the gate. Burning, bladder empties its last liquid. Mouth caked with thick detritus. Tongue swollen. Lips parched. Skin cracking. Eyes sunken in orbits. Nasal passages crusted with blood. Skin scaly. I cry, "Water!" But nobody is listening.

Two flies bother each other on the edge of the stone slab. I wait until they begin mating, swat them in their moment of distraction. I scrape my hand across my teeth and swallow drily without chewing. My throat catches but I suppress the rising bile. I lick what's left of the meal from my palm. A dry irritation remains. My throat burns.

The patient suffering dehydration can last as little as five days, as long as three weeks. I try to remember when Julia and I first met. The bar, the hospital, the basement clinic—it's all mixed up. When will I see her again? *Medianoche, puerto.* Don't let them get you, Julia.

A second night comes and goes. I weep, and with depraved satisfaction recognize the arrival of a bizarre symptom: crying without tears.

* * *

The third dawn lightens the stairs and I awaken with the oppressive sensation of a dead weight atop of me. I push it off and let out a scream, hoarse, harrowing, not my own. I climb down from the slab and feel around on the floor. There is no body, no weight, only the same scattered remains. Fever. Dry heaves. Lungs swelling.

"You stink, feo!" Always shocking me out of a shallow sleep. Throat swollen, parched. Thick secretions narrowing the respiratory tract. Difficulty breathing. Tito flicks his lighter and throws a white plastic bag with a green tourist store logo through the bars. "Brought you something to eat. I didn't have time to cook it, but I figured by now you could use the juices."

At the bottom of the bag there is a dark, pulpy mass, like cascara de guayaba. It burns for me to speak. "¿Fruta?"

"No. Es carne. A little liver I got on the parallel market. It's delicious. I thought you'd prefer it fresh. I would have brought you some bread but there's another glass scare."

I touch it. Cold.

The lighter goes out for a second and Tito flicks it again. "Pues, haz lo que te da la gana. But it's good meat. Stolen from the kitchen of the 1830. Ellos tienen las chuletas más ricas." He lights a cigarette. "Why don't you tell me where she is?"

I say nothing.

"We just want to talk with her. You won't even have to wait around. Just show me the house, and once I've seen her, you go. Maybe you can clear some of this up before it gets out of control, doctor."

"Agua."

"No water."

Esophagus contracts painfully and I can't supress a groan.

"You shouldn't complain, feo. At least it's nice and cool down here." Tito looks me in the eye. He knows he could kill me. He doesn't have a materialist concept of death. It is an abstraction, someone else's problem. "I wouldn't break my balls for her sake, doctor. At first, me and my brother were in as much trouble as you. But yesterday, divers found a scalpel at the docks where Alejandro was pushed in. It had your fingerprints on the handle, doctor."

"¿Cómo?"

"Now that nobody's seen you for a couple of days, there's quite a rumor developing around Vedado. They say you're a fag and the reason you're hiding is because you killed Alejandro in a jealous rage. Why don't you tell me where she is?"

"Hijo de—"

"All a person has to say is, 'You know the doctor in Vedado, the one with the ugly birthmark?' The rest they practically supply themselves—buggery with surgical instruments, that kind of thing." Tito climbs the stairs and calls from the top, "This is not my problem. I've given you something to eat. Understand?"

When he's gone, I consider the plastic bag, its contents. I touch it. I know there's something wrong with the meat. It's not liver, it's tough like the kidney of a pig. The size is right. Similar. I can't tell.

The scalpel: Perez could have slipped it in his overcoat the day he broke into the clinic. The black Toyota, the interview in the speakeasy—the only reason I wasn't arrested that night is because I'm bait for Julia. Perez needs us both. If I ever get out of this hell, I'll never let anyone lock me up again. Better death.

* * *

I dream of La Milagrosa and her stillborn child. She has awoken from the spell of death and found the infant nestled between her legs. Lying in the dark, she takes him and cradles him close to her breast.

"Where are we, mami?"

"What? You talking already?"

"What are those thuds, like our heartbeat but far off?"

"Shovels. Away, not overhead. Too muffled . . ."

"And that fuzzy feeling when I breathe, causing me to swallow hard?"

"It's the odor of our neighbors, the dead."

"What's this fluttering above?"

"There's something called sight, but you were not born to use it."

"And this bag in my hand?"

"My breast, long dry."

"But what's this I feel inside, where we were connected?"

"That's nothing. That's just hunger. Now think pleasant thoughts, my baby. We're going to be here a long time."

* * *

Another endless night drifting in and out of consciousness. I consider the raw meat, left untouched for hours. They are trying to get me to eat this. I will not. There is something wrong with it. I don't need it. I don't need it to live.

Why not? Just a taste. Blood is water. For the body. Have I tried it yet? Can't tell. Fingers crusted with . . . with what? Mud? Blood. Vamos, Rodriguez. Just a nibble. To live.

Out of nowhere a hole opens in the wall. Two holes: tunnels of fire, two beautiful, blazing chutes leading deep into the earth. I could take one. I could crawl over and into one or the other and be gone, out of here. The fires sear my brain. The holes become eyes. Death has a face.

In the distance I hear a child—a picnic in the cemetery, at night? My mind knows it must be a joke, but it lets my body believe: bread, sliced pork, fried plantains, lemonade! *Come here!* I'll be right there. *You've got to see this.* I have to take a piss. *You're not going to believe it.* Believe what? Shit. *They've locked it, the assholes.* Let's go. *No. Take a look.* Can you see through? *Light a match.* There's only three left and I still want to smoke the rest of this joint. *Let's smoke it here.* This place stinks of shit. Let's go back up. *You know there's corpses in there. You can see them.* I've seen enough bones. *Whole bodies, without the heads.* Disgusting. *Dead reporters. Headless, dead reporters. Light a match.*

An angel wing rises from the floor and sweeps across the walls. It descends upon my legs, torso, and flaps in my face, a blinding beam, burning. A dry, low howl: "*¡Ya!*" My own voice, unrecognizable as human, like a sound burped from a corpse.

"¡Ai!"

"¿Qué carajo fué—?"

Loud, violent smacking: tennis shoes up stone steps.

"¡Carajo! That wasn't funny." Young boys, two of them, not the brothers.

"It wasn't me—I swear. There's someone in there."

"Let's get the fuck out of here."

"*Wait!*"

"Let's get out of here. We'll tell the grounds-keeper."

"*Get me out.*"

"Carlos, get something—that iron bar." One of them climbs the stairs and fetches a broken fence-post. The boys take turns prying the gate, gasping for air and gagging at the smell. When the chain snaps, they flee up the stairs. They don't want to be touched by a living corpse.

I have barely enough strength to unwind the chain from the bars. I climb the stairs, muscles and joints in agony, but with each step there is relief for lungs and head: fresh air, like pure oxygen compared to the foul gases I've been breathing. At the top of the stairs, although the glass door is open, I am paralyzed by terror. I tell myself this is a trauma response, but I am unconsoled. The reflex is to run back down, but that is lunacy. I must step out into whatever might be next. The boys made it; so can I. I catch my breath, shift one stiff leg in front of the other, and emerge into the antechamber. Nobody. I am alone.

I stumble out of the crypt. The night is clear and I use the sliver of moon rising in the east to orient myself. It's a long walk back to the gate. I rest every few steps to catch my breath and massage the cramps out of my legs. I stop at the fountain for water, no more than a sip or I'll shock my system. I vomit. I wait, measuring the minutes by the far-off sounds of cars braking and accelerating at the signal on Zapata. I drink another ounce and hold it down this time. Tito could come anytime and I have to get out of the cemetery, but I can't go to the police. All I have now is my freedom. I will have to make choices: where to run, which way to take. Little decisions now have major consequences. I can't go by the attic or try to retrieve the Lada. I am hunted. Somewhere in this city they are breathing, the people responsible for killing Alejandro. Somewhere in this city Julia is hiding. *Medianoche, puerto.*

There is little traffic on Zapata. It is 2, maybe 3 in the morning. I wait until the street is empty and cross to the closed cafeteria. In the alley behind the kitchen I dig through a trash barrel and find a can of orange cola, nearly empty. I need ORS solution, but I have to settle for a swallow of soft drink. The sugar throws a switch in my brain: I must go to the terminal. If I can get a botero to take me out of Havana before daybreak, I might be able to find Emilio in Pinar, arrange for a boat, and be back at the Port of Havana by midnight. Then Julia and I can escape this nightmare. I find a bunch of dead flowers in the trash. Through the cemetery would be the shortest route, but there is no way I'm going back in there. I follow the wall of the necropolis up the hill, holding the bouquet of withered flowers in front of my face like an insane suitor or a demented mourner.

At the top of the hill I turn right down Paseo. The median is conspicuous, but halfway between the footpath and the roadway there are palms and palmettos in regular sequence where I can keep in the shadows. At el Patio de Maria a late rock concert has let out, and a pack of teenagers leaving the club meets me on the median. "¡Vaya, pendejo!" spits a tall one holding a Tropicola can. My bad odor and a glimpse of my crazed expression make the kid move away. "Está loco!" the boy calls to his friends, five of them.

I pull a twenty-dollar bill from the roll in my pants and hold it up to catch the pale light of the streetlamp. "Veinte dolares—sell me your baseball cap."

"Is that twenty Americano?"

"Sí. And give me what's left in that can you're drinking."

The boy takes off the hat and throws it on the ground. He drinks one more swallow from the can and sets it down beside the hat. "Throw the money down."

I crumple up the bill and toss it at the teenager, who fumbles with it for a second and shouts to his friends, "¡Vámonos!" They part ranks and scramble wide around me as if I were a leper. Their laughter dies away all down Paseo.

I put the baseball cap on and taste the canned cocktail, permitting myself just one sip: awful, luke-warm cola cut with chispe tren, but the alcohol takes only a few seconds to administer a calming, anesthetic effect. I pull the hat low over my eyes, hold the flowers against my cheek, and resume the march down Paseo toward the Plaza de la Revolución. Before getting too close to the monument, I cut left to the Teatro Nacional, where I stop to drink from the fountain, then out toward Boyeros and the National Library, a shortcut to the bus terminal.

I stop at the treeline and sip the last of the cola cocktail, peering across the street at the taxi stand. There are no boteros leaving long-distance at this hour, but five private taxis lined up at the curb await delayed arrivals. On the steps of the terminal, four drivers stand chattering and stretching their legs. At the end of the line of cars, the last driver is asleep in his front seat. Silently I cross the street and rap lightly on his half-lowered window. He awakens with a start. "¡Coño que susto!"

"Llévame para Pinar y te doy cien dólares Americanos."

The driver's black guayabera is stained from front-seat meals. He is groggy but sensible enough to keep his voice down so his competitors don't hear the negotiation. "You smell like a pig."

"I'll sit in back." I dig in my pocket and hold up the roll of money.

"I can smell you from here."

"Stop at the Teatro Nacional and I'll wash off in the fountain."

The driver looks at the money, frowns, and jerks

his chin toward the backseat. "Get in quickly." I crack the back door and slip in. "Don't slam it. Hold the handle. Keep your head down until I get away from these sinvergüenzas." He starts the car and pulls out into the road. "¡Hasta mañana!" he calls to the drivers on the steps.

One of them shouts back, "¡Sueña con los mariconcitos!"

"Okay, shut the door now," the driver says. "¿Qué te pasó a ti?"

I rise from the floor but stay slumped in the seat, the hat brim pulled down over my brow. "M'emboraché."

"¡Échale!" he says at the thought of a good drunk.

The driver pulls up in front of the fountain. I get out, remove my filthy clothes, and wash off. When I put the dirty rags back on, the smell makes me gag. I vomit on the trunk of a royal palm.

Shortly before dawn, we are at the outskirts of Havana when the driver slows for a fat woman at a parasombra. I protest, "Wait, no more passengers. I'm paying you to rent the whole car."

"She's not a passenger, compañero. Es mi prima. Familia. Sube aquí en frente si quieres."

I move to the front seat and he helps the woman fill the back with her bags and baskets. The driver pulls onto the highway and for a mile all is silent.

The sun is beginning to rise above the hills to the west. I am exhausted, ready to allow myself a short nap, when in the rearview mirror I see the fat woman gawking back at my mark on my cheek. She screams, "¡Para! ¡Para la máquina!"

The driver slams on the brakes. "¡Coño! ¿Qué pasa, vieja?"

"¡Asesino! ¡Mounstro!" she shouts. "Mató a ese chulo."

The driver casts about frantically and sees my lunar. "¡Sí! ¡Es él!" he cries. He reaches in the ashtray and pulls out a little knife, pointing it at me. "Butcher! Get out of here!" I throw the door open and jump out of the car. The driver speeds away, rear wheels spitting gravel. The day is dawning. I have to get out of the light.

I follow the alleys to Yorki's apartment at the outskirts of Vedado and find the spare key under the Santa Barbara outside his door. A look in the bedroom: nobody home. I use his phone to call Emilio's place in Pinar. No answer. I fall asleep on the sofa and dream I am back down in the hole, my shoulders against the cold slab.

I awaken to the sun high above the rooftops. Yorki's living room window is open to the squeals of children playing in the street below. I reach for the phone and call Emilio's, letting it ring for a long time.

A key suddenly turns in Yorki's front door and I put down the phone. It's Yorki, alone. "¡Coño qué susto!" He shuts the door and puts his sunglasses on the shelf. "Are you all right?"

"What day is it?"

"Friday." Friday: three days underground without food or water. Tomorrow Emilio will be heading out on his solo patrol. "You look awful. Sit down. Let me get you some coffee."

"You have coffee?"

Yorki disappears into the kitchen and comes back with two tasas of strong, sugary café, cold. "I'm heating up a new pot. ¡Coño! You look even worse than usual." He cracks the door and peeks down the hall, then closes it and says in a low voice, "Why haven't you come forward to defend yourself?"

"It's not true what they're saying. I'm being set up."

"The PNR came by yesterday to question me. And the CDR has been watching this block. It's not safe for you to be here, Mano."

"I just need until dark. Por favor . . ."

"Of course. Forgive me, Mano. Don't think about it. You'll get this thing straightened out. The important thing is that you're okay. We were worried about you."

"¿Como está Carlota?"

Yorki looks out the window. "Pretty shaken up.

Her neighbors are saying crazy things. She told Pablo you went to Miami for a vacation. He wants you to bring him back an apple."

"He's always wanted to try an apple. Yorki, do you have any cigarettes?"

"Sure." He takes a pack from the table and lights one, hands it to me.

"Marlboro. Terrible." I take one puff and stub it out. "Do you have anything to eat? A little rice?"

"I'll heat up some chícharo." Yorki disappears into the kitchen.

"You don't have to heat it." I lie on the sofa and let my gaze drift out the living room window all the way to the Microbrigade Buildings, the ugly ex-Soviet embassy towers in Miramar. A mother calls names in the street: ¡Vladi! ¡Niurka! ¡Manuel! Feeling dizzy, I swirl my tongue around the bottom of the coffee cup to lick up the last of the sugary grounds. I realize the street has gone silent. The children have stopped playing. "Yorki?" He doesn't answer.

I get up from the sofa and peer into the kitchen: empty, and Yorki has left the window open onto the street below. A small posse of women has gathered outside the entrance to the apartment house. Seeing me, one of them cries, "¡Allí 'stá!" I duck back inside and turn the bedroom doorknob, but Yorki has locked himself in. Hijo de puta betrayed me without even looking me in the eye.

I grab Yorki's sunglasses from the living room shelf when the front door sways open and my stomach tenses. A sturdy man stands in the doorway. "Doctor? I'm here to help."

Another man holding a baseball bat comes up behind the first. "You're a prize catch!"

"You'll go straight to the hospital and they'll fix you up. Our government is fair. You'll get a trial."

"Just like Ochoa did," says the man with the bat.

I won't let them lock me up again. I dive head-first out Yorki's window onto the roof of the front portal. The men come after me and I jump twelve feet to the grass, the shock stinging my legs, a few feet away from the knot of neighborhood women. "¡Cuidado! ¡Es él!" one of them cries.

"That's right," I growl, "I'm the murderer. And I'll kill you like I did that chulo." The women scatter. I hear the shouts of the men clambering down the front stairway and run around the back of the building. I hop on Yorki's moped, run it down the alley, start it with a kick, and weave through the back streets of Vedado, leaving the man with the baseball bat swinging in the dust. I slip on Yorki's sunglasses and ride down Paseo ahead of the shouts echoing from the balconies.

Shaking from the adrenaline, I hide the moped in the ruins of an abandoned building behind Cine

Chaplin. During the darkness of a crowded matinee, I enter through the broken back door of the theater and collapse in a front-row chair: *Fresa y chocolate*.

The flickering screen and the breathing of the other moviegoers momentarily soothes my rattled nerves. I am here among other people, where I belong. I am not a monster. I am a man, a doctor. Maybe it would have been easier if my mother had taken me down that hole with her. It probably would have been much easier.

Eyelids grow heavy and begin to shut, but I can't allow myself to sleep here. When the credits roll I head to the bathroom to sit in a stall before the lights go up. When the next showing begins, I dig in the trash and find a can with a little cola left and a paper cone with a few peanuts. I return to my seat, chewing and sipping slowly.

I wait agonizingly through four screenings, keeping an eye on the glowing clock on the wall. When I leave the theater at 11:30, I ride Yorki's moped east along the Malecón to the end. The skies over the straits are dark with ominous stormclouds. The moon and stars remain hidden. I hide the moped between tall stacks of loading pallets and slip through a gap in the fence that circles the Port of Havana.

This side of the harbor is an iron graveyard. Hulking boxcars blackened with soot lie dormant on disused tracks. If this is where she's hiding out, it's been as poor a way to pass the week as my own. "¿Hola?" The sound of tide washing over dead coral. Distant laughter carries across the channel from a cruise ship bedecked with colored lanterns. "Julia?"

She steps out of the shadows carrying a purse. When I walk toward her she holds a finger to her lips. Standing a few inches from her, I can smell her skin. "I'm in trouble," I say.

"You're in it deeper than me." She gives me a peculiar smile. "A girlfriend told me about the sorts of things they've been saying around Vedado since you got locked up."

"You knew I was down there?"

"Tito got the word out through the girls in Havana that you didn't have any water and would probably die within seventy-two hours. He was playing cat-and-mouse to try and get me to come out. But today he got a tip to look for me here."

Laughter reaches us from the cruise ship and Julia pulls something from her purse. My throat catches. She is holding a small Russian pistol. "Where did you get that?"

"He came ready to defend himself against a knife, but it never occurred to him that I might have Alejandro's gun . . ."

I almost step on him, legs sticking out from behind the last boxcar. It's dark, but it was dark down in the crypt and I recognize the sneakers and pants of the man who held me captive. A wave of nausea washes over me. Tito's head lies severed on the other side of the rail.

"I'll need your help dragging him the rest of the way." She lifts his feet and nods for me to take the shoulders. "He's heavier than Alejandro."

I have to call upon a reserve of surgeon's equilibrium to speak. "No."

"¡Carajo, Mano! You can't do things halfway."

"Stop this, Julia. You're sick."

"There were two ways this could have ended, but you've given me no choice." Her face contorts the way it did when she hit me with the ashtray, except that now she's pointing a gun at me. "A wealthy foreigner is going to get me out, a diplomat."

"One of your johns?"

"Shut up. You're in no position to judge me. All the jineteras spoke of the doctor who'd give the test for AIDS without asking their name, but you never slept with them. Why is that? You pretend it's for your socialismo, pero I knew better before I even met you. You're sentimental: You believe in love. En fin, you're stupid. All I had to do was shake my tail in your face long enough and I knew you'd break down."

She levels her hand and points the pistol straight at my gut.

"Wait, Julia!"

"Go to hell. You don't even know my real name."

I stagger to the sea wall and jump at the crack of the first shot—the shock of the water and I don't know whether I've been hit. More shots, and I dive, swimming beneath the surface until my lungs burn.

When I come up for air, I see flashing lights in the railyard. I climb out on the rocks and all four doors open on a dark Mercedes parked at the sea wall: three men in olive-green and Perez in an overcoat. "Hello, doctor. Get in."

I sit shivering in back between two of the khakied guards. When Perez puts me in prison, I'll make it a short stay. I learned in medical school that it's not very difficult to end your life with a few simple tools: a plastic bag, a shoestring, a damp cloth. I won't ever let them lock me up again.

We're speeding down the Malecón when the driver turns at 23rd Street. He parks in front of my house. "Such a pity," Perez says, turning to face me from the passenger seat of the Mercedes, "a house like this in your family so long. It must have upset you awfully when they gave the best part to that spy downstairs." The guard to my right gets out of the car. Perez explains, "I'll take you to the hospital, if you wish, but you'd probably rather get out here."

"You're letting me go? But all of Vedado thinks I'm a killer."

"No te preocupas. Your neighbors have been informed."

"Informed?"

"We've told the CDR woman of your innocence. A false lead made you a suspect. By morning all Havana will know we caught the real killer—the jinetera. Come by the PNR tomorrow night and we'll take your testimony."

I am dropped off to a blackout. I climb the stairs and lock the attic door. No running water, but I have enough in three-gallon jugs to bathe with a sponge. Before I can dry off, I collapse on the sofa in absolute exhaustion and sleep.

22 August 1992

In the morning the rain starts falling and the attic is subject to the glares of everyone in the neighborhood. Between cups of chamomile tea and fits of sleep, I crack the door and hear Beatrice talking about me on the phone, *que siempre era raro, un médico perverso.* Nobody will ask how I got the lunar anymore. It will be associated with something else. Even if I'm not going to rot in jail, I've ruined my personal and professional reputations. Everything: my record as a pediatrician, the attic apartment, the roll of American twenties—everything is worthless.

I make tea and tune into Radio Reloj. "*Meteorologists are closely monitoring the first major tropical storm of the season . . .*" The city is bracing for a hurricane and the blackout might stretch for days. I lie down again and sleep through the afternoon.

* * *

Night arrives with a violent wind as the rain becomes a drenching downpour. Everyone has taken shelter inside. I turn up the collar of my raincoat and head down the service stairs. I walk to the filling station on Malecón, buy a liter of gas, and press on through the crashing waves to Miramar. I find the Lada where I left it and drive it across the Puente la Lisa, splashing through the flooded streets of Vedado to PNR headquarters.

Perez sits across from me at his desk. I tell him everything I know, but he already knows it all and much more. "After you pulled that trick with the skeleton in your window," Perez says, his gray apparatchik eyes wearily twinkling, "I exerted a bit of psychological pressure on Tito by arresting his brother as a prime suspect. I held Jochi because he's older and can get the maximum penalty—that's what I told Tito. But also because Jochi was clearly the weaker-willed brother. All I needed to do was ask Tito if he had seen you because I hoped you could lead us to the jinetera. But he surprised me by disappearing himself—hiding out at the necropolis, it turns out." The buzz of the air conditioner seems to get louder when Perez adds, "Yesterday we found Alejandro's head in a vat of acid at a Palo Monte church." He pours me some brandy from a decanter. "They struggled, fought, and she stabbed him repeatedly with the scalpel. The girl dragged his body a little more than five meters and laid his neck under the wheel of the last boxcar on a freight train. Then she uncoupled the car from the end of the freight and released the brake, same as she did to Tito after she shot him last night. Friday afternoon my men were at the railyard collecting evidence, so the response was quick when gunfire was reported just before midnight. It turns out the foreigner who had been sheltering her is a rather high-ranking diplomat."

"What will happen to him?"

"There are many varieties of crime, doctor. I make it my profession to puzzle over just one." Perez turns away and gazes out the windshield at the Swiss Embassy. "I'll transfer her to the juvenile justice division at the end of the week. If you want you can see her first."

I don't know whether it's more morbid to say that I do or I don't. If I do, it's because I want to look at the face of a teenage girl who could have done what she did. If I don't, it's because I want to preserve unspoiled the image of an innocent jinetera I laid down with. She was right about some things. Sentimental people are easy to fool.

At home alone in my attic, I light a cigarette and turn on the TV. They are showing *Memorias del subdesarrollo* on Canal 6. I treat myself to a Shiraz that Director González dropped off while I was out.

I glance at El Ché but he still isn't speaking to me. There is a bitter, bilious taste on my tongue, and the wine doesn't seem quite right. I flick the knob before Corrieri can stick his head in his wife's forsaken stocking, and I fall asleep on the sofa.

23 August 1992

By midnight the edge of Huracán Andrés is upon
the island. Lightning flashes illuminate the curtains, but the howling wind drowns out the thunder:
wet, dark gusts at the edge of a storm a hundred
miles wide. Radio Reloj says I should get down to
street level, but I've weathered several major storms
up here in the attic with just El Ché and the spirit
of Aurora. The light of the gas stove will be enough
to read by. I'll pass the hurricane in the middle of
my room, crouched at the edge of the sofa, sipping
pretend coffee in the dark, reveling in the symphony
of the winds.

There's a rapping at the French doors. I am
ready to pin it on the gale, but it continues, rhythmically. I touch the latch and feel it jiggle. I jerk away
my trembling hand. My nerves have been shot since
the time in the tomb. I light a cigarette. Even as I try

to assuage my alarm with reason, I struggle against the impulse to throw open the doors, let in the wind and rain, expose the balcón. I am inches away from the source of the rapping. Cold water leeches in under the French doors and my feet are naked. The wind suddenly blows the doors open with a slam and books and clothes fly out the window in the vacuum. I stumble backwards and the edge of the coffee table catches the back of my skull. Blacking out, I see a figure on the balcón silhouetted by lightning. All is absorbed.

24 August 1992

Twelve resounding clangs as the bell of the old Episcopalean church marks the forward march of hours—or is it tolling backwards?

"You got knocked out. What a mess!" Director González stands over me straightening the books on the shelf. He sizes up the small attic, shakes his head, and says, "This is a place where wine is drunk in swigs."

"¿Qué?"

"Those empty bottles in piles by the door. They all have the corks plugged in them."

"How long have you been here?"

"I just arrived. But the storm is almost twelve hours gone." Director González reaches into his pocket for a metal flask. "Want some whiskey?"

"No. Not yet."

He says, "Go ahead, Rodriguez," and so I do.

"Sorry about the awful trouble you went through. And now this . . ." Wet clothes, books, and papers are strewn all over the floor.

"What's the damage like down there?"

"What you'd expect: many trees and poles blown down, trash all over the streets, flooding along the Malecón. If you're feeling all right you should get downstairs. There are people waiting outside the clinic, many distressed and some with minor injuries. A few will need sedatives. Most just want ibuprofen. Get yourself some too."

"The clinic doesn't have any of that."

"It does now."

"How?"

"Colonel Perez took care of it." On his way out the door Director González says, "Get down there, Rodriguez. Vedado needs you."

I head down and open the clinic. On the street everyone is talking about Andrés and its aftermath. All are glad to be outdoors. Nobody likes being trapped, even in his own home, even for one night. Radio Reloj says that Cuba was spared the worst. The eye tore right across Florida and Miami has been devastated. There is no way of knowing the total casualties at sea, but it would have been very hard for anyone out on the Florida Straits in a small craft.

* * *

For two straight days I see walk-ins at all hours and monitor trauma patients in the cots overnight. On the third day, a nurse spells me for a couple of hours and I walk through flooded streets along the Malecón. The houses and apartments of Vedado had already been in ruins—roofs corroding, balconies crumbling, unpainted walls riddled with cracks that sprout hideous branches and vines—and after a flood leaving behind only moderate additional damage, everything somehow looks more vibrant than before.

There's no contact allowed in the interview room at PNR headquarters. She wears a gray uniform, looking tired, drawn, nothing like the girl who brought me a ham sandwich from the Habana Libre.

"I didn't mean to kill Alejandro."

"I know." I light a cigarette and look over at the guard. He nods and I hand it to her. Her touch, briefly lingering, feels dead to me. I light another cigarette for myself.

"While you went to visit your family in Pinar, he sent another jinetera over to arrange a meeting at the bottom of the Malecón, where they dock the ships. I was supposed to pay him off. He wanted needles, pills, whatever I could get from your polyclinic. There wasn't anything, but I brought the scalpel—the one you used in the kitchen—to scare him and to protect myself. He said very cruel things and we fought. He laughed when I showed him the scalpel. I cut him just once in the neck. But the blood—it was awful."

"Don't think about it."

"I was starting to change. I could feel it changing in me, and he was dragging me back down."

I don't contradict her. She's just a child. She's going to have to live with this a long time.

"Time's up," says the guard.

"I love you, Mano. I know you don't believe me."

Walking out of PNR headquarters onto Havana's flood-ravaged streets, maybe I do believe her. Alejandro wouldn't let her go. She was trapped in the world of the jinetera. So she clawed to get out, thrust the scalpel into him to break the lock.

Back in Vedado, Habaneros are drying rugs, towels, and papers on their patios. At least now, in the water's retreat, there's salt. In the flooded neighborhoods, they're scraping it off the walls. If it hadn't been for the storm, I might have remained the monster, the derelict, but now I'm becoming the doctor again. I return home to pick through the debris in my own attic. Beneath a pile of my scattered books I uncover the tattered poster of El Ché. That's where I find the photos Elena loaned her palero, hiding behind El Ché, taped to his back. The lunar is on my right cheek in the print, on my left in the reverse-positive, white like a crescent moon. I walk them down to the Malecón. In Vedado, across from where the baseball fields used to be, that's where I take El Ché and the conflicted young man with the stain on his face. I cast them off to the Florida Straits and they float face-up on the surface of the water. The evening is bright and clear—a perfect night to walk along the Malecón.

Also available from Akashic Books

FAST EDDIE, KING OF THE BEES
a novel by Robert Arellano
236 pages, trade paperback original, $13.95

"A tight close-up, mile-a-minute monkey-cam with more word plays than Eminem."
—Arthur Nersesian, author of
The Sacrificial Circumcision of the Bronx

"A Dickensian journey on speed . . . bizarrely picaresque and wittily ribald . . . deliriously funny."
—*Providence Journal*

DON DIMAIO OF LA PLATA
a novel by Robert Arellano
200 pages, trade paperback original, $13.95

"A former student of Robert Coover, Arellano has created a brilliant novel of political satire based on an actual mayoral stint in Providence, RI . . . Recommended for all fiction collections." —*Library Journal*

"A raucously funny satire of machine politics wrapped up in a parody of *Don Quixote*." —*Chicago Reader*

SOUTH BY SOUTH BRONX
a novel by Abraham Rodriguez
292 pages, trade paperback original, $15.95

"A street poet like Bob Dylan, Rodriguez has woven a lyrically inventive and sophisticated noir . . . Full of unforgettable one liners, *South by South Bronx* manages to film a neighborhood filled with beauty, danger, and magic. One fearless, hell of a literary mystery novel."
—Ernesto Quiñonez, author of *Bodega Dreams*